LINEAR TACTICAL SERIES

OUTLAW

USA TODAY BESTSELLING AUTHOR
JANIE CROUCH

CODE NAME: OUTLAW

This book is dedicated to my brother-in-law, Mark… 1/3 of the original Outlaws.
And to Kim, who puts up with him.

Chapter 1

Jenna Franklin stood staring out the window of her house in western Wyoming, eyes frozen on the breathtaking scenery in front of her.

Staring out at the Grand Tetons wasn't unusual. Most of the people who came to the more remote section of this state did so because of the mountain range and national park. They wanted to hike in warm weather or ski in the cold. Or just enjoy the vast blue sky above and the greenery all around them.

God's country. Western Wyoming had been called the closest thing to heaven on earth by more than one person.

Right now, Jenna called it closer to hell.

Although, granted, it wasn't the Tetons' fault. Anywhere outside was the equivalent to hell for Jenna.

Just standing at the window was enough to make her breathing grow more labored and turn her palms clammy. It was all she could do not to back away from the beautiful scenery assaulting her eyes.

She knew she was safe here. This was Oak Creek. She had dozens of friends living all around this area.

And not just regular friends, *warrior* friends. Former Special Forces soldiers who'd come home to create Linear Tactical—a self-defense and survival training school to teach civilians the skills they'd honed in the military—friends.

And their wives, who were just as badass as the former soldiers themselves.

Jenna had friends all around this tiny town, almost all of whom knew what she had survived and would do anything to help her. This had to be the safest place on the planet for her.

But still, standing here knowing she needed to go outside had her stomach clenching so hard she might vomit on the floor.

It didn't matter that she logically knew outside posed no real threat to her.

Outside was the enemy. Outside would choke the life out of her. Outside would…

No.

She couldn't let that line of thought take over. She'd been back in Oak Creek nearly three weeks, and she hadn't forced herself outside once. That was a new low even for her.

This had to end today. If she kept losing ground, how long until she'd lose herself completely?

She needed to go outside.

Exposure therapy. That's what her multiple psychiatrists called it. Going outside a little bit at a time, until one day, maybe outside wouldn't be terrorizing at all.

Today was definitely not that day.

Her nails gripped into the soft wood of the window frame. Five minutes. That was all she was asking of herself— to go out for five minutes. Three hundred seconds.

She had to go outside today. She couldn't lose yet another day to the irrational fears that tried to control her mind.

Jenna stepped back from the window, but she knew better than to try going straight out the front door. That would be a disaster. Instead, she marched into her garage, not stopping until she was inside her car. She sat inside it without starting it, letting her rapid heart rate ease a little.

Her car was also a safe place. On the outside, it looked like a regular mid-range SUV. But it was fortified in ways that most normal people wouldn't ever even think about: bulletproof glass, anti-hijack doors that no one could open except for her once she was inside, anti-slash tires. Her vehicle was a safe place.

But she couldn't stay here. She needed *out* of a safe place. The sound of her own heartbeat thrashed in her ears as she punched in the code to open her garage door.

Then she pulled the car out to the end of her short drive-way. For anyone watching, it would seem absurd that she was sitting in her car doing nothing—neither leaving nor going back inside.

Just sitting there, paralyzed.

Her grip on the steering wheel made her knuckles white. She finally forced herself to let go and reach for the handle of the door. Her teeth chattered and her fingers shook as she punched in the code that would open it.

Jenna had to do this now or she wasn't going to do it at all.

Five minutes. She would stand in her driveway for five damned minutes. She could survive anything for that short amount of time.

She heard her watch automatically start timing as she stepped outside of the car. It would beep when her torture session was complete.

She closed the door but kept a hand on her vehicle as everything began spinning around her. She made it ten

3

seconds before her breakfast ended up vomited on the pavement.

She reached for the car door, desperate to escape this torment, but then stopped. She had to do this. Five minutes.

She forced herself to complete one of the grounding mechanisms a therapist had given her to ward off panic attacks.

List five things you can see.

She could barely see anything with her eyes so runny from the vomiting, but she completed the exercise.

She could see the mountains.

The blue sky.

Her car. The house. Her...feet.

Whatever, it still counted.

List four things you can hear.

Her breathing. It was hard to hear anything over her breathing. She held her breath for just a second and found she could hear other things.

A bird.

And then maybe a car off in the distance.

That was only three, but it was close enough.

Three things you can touch.

She touched her own shoulder. Okay.

The car. Okay.

The mailbox was only a few steps away. She could touch that too. She let go of the car and walked toward the mailbox.

Mistake.

Immediately, pressure slammed into Jenna's chest, making it impossible to breathe. Her fingers ripped at her throat, but she couldn't get any air in.

Don't fool yourself into thinking you're ever going to get out of here.

Jenna pushed her hands over her ears, but it didn't help.

The voices were inside her head—covering her ears wasn't going to stop them. She stumbled back toward the car.

You will do exactly what we tell you to do, or you will discover there are worse things than dying.

Fists. Kicks. Curling into a ball and trying to survive.

She fell hard against the car. The world was blacking out around her as she was swallowed by the past. If she didn't get inside her vehicle in the next few seconds, she wouldn't make it inside at all.

A broken jaw. Concussion. This guy is going to be eating out of a straw for quite a while.

She let out a low moan with the oxygen she had left. No, that was even worse. She couldn't think about that.

She punched in the code on the driver's side door, getting it wrong the first time. Damn it, she had to concentrate; there was only a one-time grace period. She focused all her waning attention on the keypad and typed in the code again.

Maybe the animals will finish you off this time. We'll see if you're still alive tomorrow.

She let out a sob as the locks clicked, and she yanked the door open, diving into the seat. As soon as she pulled the door closed behind her, some of the pressure eased, and she felt like she could breathe again. At least enough to keep herself from passing out.

She lay there, head wrapped in her arms as she tried to reclaim actual reality, *real* reality, not the dizzying blend of past and present and hell.

When she could finally control herself enough to pull into the garage and lower the door behind her, she looked down at her watch. It had automatically stopped timing when she'd gotten back inside the car. Surely she had made it to close to five minutes.

Fifty-eight seconds.

All that and she hadn't even made it a minute.

Jenna put her head on the steering wheel and began to cry.

Chapter 2

"Do you remember that time I had my face buried in your ass right here on this very cliff wall?"

Mark Outlawson didn't even try to stop his bark of laughter at Baby Bollinger's words. Baby had a grin on his face as he said it. Of course, Baby always had a grin on his face. He was one of the most charming and good-natured guys Mark had ever known.

Not that the face/ass situation Baby was referring to had been very funny. Baby had almost plummeted to his death when someone sabotaged his rappelling gear during an obstacle race.

"I recall you asking me to tell you if I was going to pass gas so that you could just let go and die," Riley responded with a grin of his own.

"Can you blame me?" Baby asked. "I've camped enough with you now, I know I would never survive up-close contact with one of your SBDs."

"SBD?" Riley asked.

Baby chuckled. "Silent but deadly. I'd take my chances with plummeting three stories straight down."

"Smart man," Mark muttered.

Riley Harrison, known to most of the world as daredevil television sensation *Phoenix*. If it hadn't been for Riley's exceptional reflexes and coordination, not to mention sheer determination to get his friend down to the ground safely, Baby would've died that day.

"Belay on," Ian DeRose called from a few yards above them. "Unless you'd rather stay down there and hear the story of the greatest bromance there never was."

Mark chuckled again. "I think I'll pass. Climbing!"

Mark had rock climbed with Ian, his friend and boss at Zodiac Tactical, more than once. A traditional belay would be from beneath the climber, but Mark knew Ian could more than handle it from above.

He trusted his friend enough to take a more difficult path up the cliff wall. If he fell, Ian would catch him. Mark hoisted himself up foot by foot, finding finger- and toeholds until he made it up to Ian.

They sat on a slight edge, still able to hear Baby and Riley joking below them. Mark looked out at the beautiful mountains and skies surrounding him. He'd missed being here in Wyoming.

"You took a more difficult route up." Ian's eyes were also on the stunning view.

"Worried you weren't going to be able to stop me if I fell?"

"Hell no. But maybe a little worried I'd have to explain to Dumb and Dumber down there why I had to."

Mark gritted his teeth, some of the beauty around him dimming. "I don't need a babysitter."

Ian raised an eyebrow at him. "You and I have been friends for too many years and you've saved my ass way too many times for me to ever be your babysitter. But you can't ignore what's happening."

Mark scrubbed a hand down his face. "Yeah, but it's not affecting this. Not today."

"Fair enough, Outlaw."

Outlaw. What a joke that was becoming. Everyone at Zodiac Tactical had a code name, and Outlaw was his. Partially because of his last name being Outlawson, but mostly because it had always been Mark's mantra.

He'd always been able to think outside the box, to see different ways of handling a problem than just the obvious— even back when he was in the Special Forces. Outlaw suggested rebel, but that wasn't so much the case. Mark was willing to follow orders, but he was also willing to fight with less conventional measures when needed.

That had made him quite the bodyguard after leaving the military and was one of the reasons why Ian had hired him to work at Zodiac Tactical, the world-renowned private security business he'd built.

Zodiac were the utmost experts at security work of all types: risk consulting, intelligence gathering, private and corporate guarding, international hostage negotiation and rescue.

If the law couldn't, or wouldn't, handle it, Ian DeRose and his team could. Mark had been damned proud to be part of that team for the past two years.

But soon, he and Ian would be having a hard talk. Things couldn't continue the way they had been.

"Hey." Ian nudged him. "I shouldn't have brought it up. I'm sorry."

"Don't worry about it." Mark looked out at the mountains to the north of them. "You ever miss this view when you're in New York?"

Ian had moved there when his wife Wavy's art career had taken off.

Ian shrugged. "I appreciate this more since I'm not

around it as often. But the city has its own appeal. And honestly, I would take any view as long as I know Wavy's near it."

After what had happened to her, it was still hard for Ian to be away from Wavy at all. Even to go rock-climbing while she was in town a few miles away.

"Lord, are you guys talking lovey-dovey stuff about my sister?" Baby asked as he and Riley made it the rest of the way up to them. "If so, I can once again attempt to plummet to my death."

Mark pushed himself back from the ledge so they could begin climbing again. "No, we were trying to figure out if we could climb a different section of this rock to avoid face-to-ass, good ol' days stories."

"Best day of my life." Riley grinned and started climbing past them.

From this point to the top of the cliff wall, their equipment was set up and anchored for all of them to climb without needing to spot each other. At the top was rappelling gear to get them back down.

That was the advantage of adventuring with a billionaire. They didn't have a ton of time today, so Ian had arranged for someone to set up and take down their equipment. All they had to do was enjoy the scenery, company, and the challenge.

Challenges had never been something Mark shied away from.

They all began moving up the wall. A few yards in, Mark could feel the slight drag of his left leg and bit back a curse. If the pattern held, his leg would continue to become more useless over the next few hours, then hopefully would right itself later tonight as he slept.

Doctors had warned him that at some point the rejuvenation may stop.

He would deal with that when it came to it. Right now, he was determined not to show any weakness. He knew he was succeeding when Baby and Riley began their joking with each other again. Riley climbed past Mark at a rate he'd never be able to match, current physical issues or not.

But then again, Riley was a world-class athlete and a decade younger, so Mark wasn't going to sweat it.

Riley got a little farther up, then stopped and flipped so he was almost hanging upside down like freaking Spiderman. "Don't you think it's interesting how we don't see Mark in Oak Creek for like two years until Jenna showed back up here?"

Baby and Ian both chuckled.

"Highly suspicious," Baby said.

Mark rolled his eyes. "Hey, if I haven't been around, blame my asshole boss. He's the one who keeps me out on missions all the time."

Ian chuckled, not taking offense. "Funny how you let your *asshole boss* know you needed time off as soon as Jenna Franklin resurfaced here."

They all got a little quiet. *Resurfaced* was the right word. For over a month, no one had known where she'd gone, or why she'd disappeared.

But Mark had known. He'd witnessed it.

"I'm not here because of Jenna," he said out loud. "I'm here because, evidently, I needed more jackasses in my life, and you three were readily available. Tell me what's been going on around Wyoming's most notorious town."

Riley and Baby launched into tales of what had been happening in Oak Creek as they climbed, like Mark wanted. It kept their attention off him and that he was moving a little slower than he should be.

And they had no shortage of stories to tell. With all the Linear Tactical guys and their military backgrounds and contacts, someone always seemed to be in danger or drawing some sort of trouble.

And, of course, everyone was getting married and having babies. That was happening at Zodiac Tactical too.

But it wouldn't be happening for Mark. Not with the health news he'd gotten a couple of months ago.

Mark was the last one to the top, thanks to his damned leg, but not so far behind that anyone really noticed. He rubbed at his knee and calf as the other guys took in the view around them.

He didn't want to rush them to head back down—that would definitely give away what was happening. But rappelling was heavily leg- and knee-dependent. Mark should have a few hours before his really became a problem, but he didn't want to take a chance on this being the one time the pain and numbness moved quickly through his limbs.

Ended up he was saved by a highly unlikely situation. They'd only been at the top of the cliff for a few minutes before Ian got a message on the two-way radio from one of his assistants.

"Boss, we just got word of a situation in Oak Creek."

Ian froze. "Wavy?"

"Secure. Her team has eyes on her. She's at her mom's."

Wavy had a security team everywhere she went. Ian had too many enemies who might once again try to use her to get to him. There was no way in hell Mark's boss would ever allow a repeat of that.

Ian relaxed slightly at the news his wife was okay. "What's going on?"

"We're not sure. All we know is there are weapons drawn at the Eagle's Nest. Some sort of situation involving outsiders. Dorian and Ray Lindstrom captured them on the way into town."

Mark met eyes with Ian. Everyone knew Dorian and Ray, but the husband and wife tended to keep the lowest of profiles. With their pasts, it was necessary.

If they'd taken someone into their own custody, it was a big deal.

"Any indication of what this is about?" Ian asked.

"Apparently something to do with Jenna Franklin."

Mark froze. What the hell would someone want with Jenna?

"Make sure Wavy's team keeps her out of town," Ian said. "We'll be there ASAP."

Mark was already running for the rappelling equipment.

Chapter 3

Jenna's hands were still shaking hours later as her fists pummeled the fighting dummy.

When most women referred to a BOB, it was a Battery Operated Boyfriend. But for Jenna, BOB was a Body Opponent Bag—a lifelike mannequin with a vinyl "skin" for more realistic self-defense training.

She ignored the tremor in her limbs as she struck one of the multiple BOBs in her home gym and training area. The tremors were no longer coming from fear, but from exhaustion.

She'd beat the fear out of her system after the first hour in her gym. It had melted away, leaving only anger.

Anger at what had been done to her.

Anger at the fact that she couldn't get past it and enjoy being outside.

Anger that even if she could get past it, she should probably stay inside away from people anyway.

She spun, hitting the BOB in a roundhouse kick with enough power to knock its stand off-balance, causing it to crash to the floor.

Breathing hard, she stared down at the faceless apparatus. "Sorry, buddy."

BOB didn't reply. He never did.

Jenna wiped sweat from her forehead. As always, her workout session had exhausted her enough to allow her to reset herself. At first, her training had been a mental necessity—learning how to get herself out of dangerous situations. Making sure she could never again be taken against her will.

She'd become a damned expert at that.

But having these deadly skills could lead to even more nightmares—she knew that from experience. What good was knowing how to defend yourself if you had no control?

She unstrapped her sparring gloves, wincing at the sight of her fists. The thin gloves had saved her hands from the worst of the abuse, but she was still going to have bruised and tender knuckles.

She righted BOB then spent the next few minutes cleaning up the gym. She'd brutalized three different fighting dummies and pounded the hell out of two different bags.

It still didn't change the fact that she hadn't even made it a full minute outside, but at least she was spent enough now that she didn't care.

Thirty minutes later, after a shower and with a bowl of salted caramel ice cream on the table in front of her, she cared even less.

But she grimaced when she looked down at her phone and saw she had missed half a dozen calls from Charlotte —*Charlie*—Bollinger. The tiny woman was a pit bull, and evidently, she'd discovered Jenna was in town.

Jenna let out a curse when the phone buzzed in her hand with an incoming text, this time from Wavy DeRose.

You are in Oak Creek, right? Need to talk to you.

Shit. Today was not the day Jenna wanted to have visitors, especially not ones of the good friend variety. Friends who might figure out how much she was hiding from them.

She hadn't let anyone know that she was back at her house here in town. Hell, most of her friends in Oak Creek didn't even know she owned this house.

They definitely didn't know that this house was much more than what it seemed. Sharing that information would just lead to more questions.

It was better to keep everyone at a little bit of a distance. Jenna had become an expert at that too. She wouldn't answer Wavy's text or return Charlie's call right now. Maybe they'd give up.

The doorbell rang.

Clearly, they wouldn't give up.

With a sigh, Jenna clicked the app on her phone so she could see who it was, not at all surprised to find Wavy and Charlie. She was tempted to ignore her friends, but she knew they wouldn't go away since they'd figured out she was here.

Jenna opened the door, standing so that she was as far from the outside as possible. She forced a smile on her face. "Surprise. I'm in Oak Creek."

All five-foot-one of Charlie burst through the door. She glared at Jenna with an eyebrow raised. "Hey genius, did you forget how to use your phone? I've been trying to call you for an hour."

"I was, uh, working out."

Charlie narrowed her eyes and crossed her arms over her chest. "How long have you been in Oak Creek?"

Jenna had no idea what answer would get her in the least amount of trouble. "Not very long," she finally replied.

Wavy, Charlie's much less rambunctious sister-in-law, reached over and gave Jenna a hug. "It's good to see you."

Jenna hugged her back, relieved when she could close the door.

Charlie pulled her in for a hug too. "We've missed you. You should've let us know you were in town. It's good to see your face in person rather than on a phone."

Jenna tried to pull back, but Charlie held her tight, so Jenna sank back into the hug. How long had it been since anyone had touched her?

Jenna knew exactly how long it had been, but she didn't want to think about Mark Outlawson right now.

Most people assumed Jenna was an extreme introvert because she didn't go out. But that really wasn't the case at all. Jenna liked being around people. She'd just learned to be near them through electronic channels.

And to never mention how much being alone all the time cost her. Because that would just lead to more people worrying about her when they realized she'd become such a basket case.

It was one thing to be known as the gal who didn't like to go out. It was another for everyone to know she vomited in her driveway trying to stay outside over a minute. For a year and a half, she'd kept that dirty little secret hidden.

Charlie finally pulled away, and Jenna led them toward the kitchen. "Sorry I didn't let you know I was in town. I just needed a little time."

She picked up her mostly empty ice cream bowl and put it in the sink. She looked over to find Wavy looking out the front window. This was their first time being inside Jenna's house, but they both seemed too distracted to want a tour.

"Everything okay?" Jenna asked.

Wavy turned away from the window and rolled her eyes. "My security detail is parked out front. I'm sure Ian is having a fit that I'm not still at Mom's."

"Why would Ian not want you here?" Jenna worked for Zodiac Tactical, and her boss had never had a problem with his wife coming to visit family here in Oak Creek before.

"Oh, he doesn't have a problem with me being *here*." She gave a shooing motion with her hand. "Don't worry about it. It's just Ian being overprotective."

Jenna had enough practice with being casually vague to recognize it from someone else when she heard it. "What's going on? I'm glad to see both of you, but what are you doing here?"

Her friends met each other's eyes in some sort of communication then turned back to her. "We need you to come on a field trip with us."

Oh, hell no.

Jenna fought to keep her face neutral. "I don't know that I'm really up for it today. I'm feeling a little under the weather. Sorry I didn't get your calls to save you from a wasted trip over here."

Wavy walked over and clasped her shoulder. "Seeing you, even for a few minutes, is never a wasted trip."

Jenna reached up and squeezed her hand. It would've been so easy for Wavy to hate her after everything that happened to her and Jenna's role in it, but the other woman had never cast any blame.

"Today just isn't a good day," Jenna whispered.

Charlie plopped down on a stool. "Both of us understand not having a good day."

Wavy nodded. "Sometimes I still feel like my bad days outnumber my good ones."

"We all just have to take each minute as it comes. Deal with that, then face the next minute," Charlie said. "And we all know how exhausting that can be."

Both women had survived their own ordeals. Maybe not for as long or as traumatizing as what Jenna had gone through, but they both knew what it was like to need to regroup.

"You know you can always talk to us." Wavy tucked a

strand of hair back, and Jenna caught sight of a little bit of blue paint right above her ear.

Nobody was ever surprised to see Waverly Bollinger DeRose with paint in random places on her face or body. She was one of the most famous artists in the world now. She'd taken her own tragedy and made it into beautiful art.

Why couldn't Jenna do something like that rather than beat the shit out of poor BOB?

"Sometimes talking doesn't help," she said.

Charlie shrugged. "Then you call us, and we'll sit around and *not talk*. Eat junk food. Whatever you need."

"Thank you," Jenna whispered. She wouldn't ever take them up on it, but it was really nice of them to offer.

Wavy grimaced. "But today, we're not actually here for moral support. We do need you to come with us."

Jenna shook her head. "I wasn't kidding when I said I wasn't up for a field trip. Today isn't…good."

"It's about your brother," Charlie said gently.

Jenna froze. "Craig? Is he okay? Did something happen to him?" Surely the FBI would've contacted her if the worst had happened.

She and Craig weren't as close as they probably should be, given what he'd given up to rescue her from her captivity. He'd never be an active agent for the FBI again because of the lies he'd told to help get her out. He'd been demoted to a desk job, slogging through the lowest levels of intel.

But even if they weren't close, they were still family. Someone would've notified her if he was hurt or…

"No, he's alive and unharmed," Wavy said quickly. "As a matter of fact, he's here in Oak Creek. He's at the Eagle's Nest."

Jenna relaxed a little knowing Craig was okay, but it still didn't make sense. "I don't understand. Why is he here?"

"He's here to talk to you."

Jenna grabbed her phone. There were no messages or missed calls from Craig. "Why wouldn't he let me know he's here? Why didn't he call or come here?"

She'd never invited her brother here, but hell, he worked for the FBI; surely he could get her address.

Wavy looked at Charlie. "Um, he was probably planning to come here, but then…got sidetracked. So, he's at the Eagle's Nest and would like for you to come there."

Jenna glanced back and forth between her two friends. "What is going on you're not telling me?"

Charlie stood and rolled her eyes. "Look, Ray Lindstrom spotted your brother coming into town, and she got a little freaked out about it. You know Ray, she has trust issues."

And the fact that Craig had been willing to trade Ray—a wanted fugitive—in to the authorities in order to help get Jenna out of her captivity meant that Ray didn't like Craig very much.

"So, she took him to the Eagle's Nest?" Jenna asked. Why would Ray take Craig to a bar?

Wavy winced. "Sort of. She's actually holding him at gunpoint at the Eagle's Nest."

"Well, crossbow-point," Charlie chimed in. "You know, because it's Ray."

To say the woman was good with a crossbow was an understatement. As a matter of fact, the last time Ray had seen Craig, she'd shot him with said crossbow.

Wavy took Jenna's hand. "Craig says he's here to talk to you about something official, but she won't let him go until you come and confirm that."

Shit. It looked like Jenna was going to have to go outside again after all.

Chapter 4

Charlie and Wavy both offered to drive or to ride with her, but Jenna refused. She was going to need to focus on keeping herself together, and she didn't want to have to try to chat at the same time.

As she got dressed, she could hear Wavy on the phone having pretty strong words with Ian about being overprotective. Evidently, her husband didn't want Wavy anywhere near the Eagle's Nest. But Wavy wasn't having any of it.

Jenna couldn't worry too much about Ray and her crossbow until she managed to actually get inside the bar. Facing crossbows seemed so much more surmountable than going outside.

She walked back out to the kitchen. "Okay, I'm ready. I'll meet you guys there."

Her friends both nodded and headed out the door. Jenna made her way to the garage, getting into her car. She grabbed the stress ball from the center console and squeezed the life out of it over and over. It didn't help her tension, but at least it gave her hand something to do.

She rechecked the car doors were locked, even though

she knew she didn't need to—they locked immediately upon her entrance into the vehicle—and finally forced herself to open the garage door. She put down the stress ball and backed her car out. Wavy and Charlie's vehicle, followed by Wavy's security detail, was already heading into town.

Jenna focused on breathing exercises during the short drive to the Eagle's Nest. All she had to do was get from her car into the building and she would be okay. She'd been inside the bar before, was familiar with it, knew what to expect.

The problem was the damned parking lot. It was over to the side of the building, around the corner from the front door. Would take the average person twenty to thirty seconds to get from their car to the inside of the building.

Twenty to thirty seconds.

After what she'd already put herself through today between her failed attempt to go outside and the massive workout…Jenna honestly wasn't sure she would make it.

And if she did, everybody was going to know something was really wrong. More than just nervous-for-her-brother wrong.

When they got to the bar, Jenna decided to skip the parking lot altogether. She pulled her vehicle all the way up to the front until she was almost blocking the door.

If she got a ticket, she would gladly pay it.

She didn't waste time, knowing sitting there would just make her anxiety worse. As soon as she turned off the engine, she opened the car door and ran for the door of the bar.

She kept her focus lasered on the "Yeah, we're open!" sign hanging in the glass. It was only a few feet away. The world spun around her, and all she could hear was her own breathing as she staggered toward those words. She made it, grabbing the handle and thrusting herself inside the building.

If it had been another five feet, she wouldn't have—she'd be balled on the ground outside, sobbing.

But she'd made it. She leaned back against the door, closing her eyes, taking deep breaths. *She'd made it.*

She opened her eyes and found everyone in the bar looking at her.

Not that too many people were there. Jenna recognized all of them. The Eagle's Nest's owner, Lexi, and her husband, Gavin Zimmerman, were standing behind the bar. Zac Mackay, owner and leader of Linear Tactical, was on a stool at the far end of the room. Finn Bollinger, Charlie's husband, was next to him.

They were all sitting casually. Way too casually.

Zac gently tilted his head toward a corner booth. Jenna followed his gaze and found her brother sitting beside Omega Sector agent Callum Webb. Zodiac Tactical had worked with him on more than one occasion.

Across from the two men sat a pregnant Ray, her crossbow on the table pointing in their direction, her hand resting on the trigger. At her shoulder stood Ray's husband, Dorian—the huge man looking just as *calm* as everyone else in the room.

"See?" Lexi said from behind the bar. "Jenna is here. Now we can all put our weapons away."

The crossbow was the only weapon Jenna could see, but she had no doubt there were more within reach of damned near everyone in the building.

"What is going on?" Jenna asked, taking in deep breaths to erase the rest of her dizziness. At least everyone was so caught up in this showdown that they weren't aware of her issues. "I feel like I walked into the OK Corral."

Before anyone could answer, Charlie and Wavy burst

through the door, Wavy's security team basically on top of them.

Zac cursed and stood up. "Everybody, stay calm."

The tension in the room ratcheted up a dozen notches.

"Woman, what part of *don't come in here* did you not understand?" Finn asked his wife.

Charlie glared at him, hands going to her hips. "You and I have been married how long, and you think I'm just going to sit in the *goddamned car* while my friend comes into a potentially dangerous situation?"

Finn scrubbed his hand down his face. Jenna held up a hand to stop him from whatever argument he was about to make.

She looked over at the booth. Craig didn't seem injured, but he did look pretty pale. "What's going on, Ray? You know that's my brother, right?"

"I found him wandering around town." Ray's eyes didn't leave the men across from her. "Last time I found your brother wandering around town, he was willing to sacrifice me to law enforcement. I'm a mother now. Have two kids who call me Mom and another on the way. So, you'll understand that I'm not going to take any chances this time."

Jenna walked slowly toward the booth. "Last time Craig was in town, he was doing whatever he had to in order to get me out of hell. I don't know that he would've really turned you in, but if he had, it would've been for good reason."

"Speaking of last time, can I remind you that you shot me with that fucking crossbow of yours?" Craig nodded toward the weapon on the table.

Ray's icy blue eyes narrowed. "We don't like people sneaking around, then or now. You still have full movement of all your limbs, right? Count yourself lucky."

Craig fell silent, but Callum leaned back next to him in the booth. His hands weren't visible under the table, which probably meant he had a gun pointed at Ray. "Dorian, why don't you get your wife under control. She's got a weapon pointed at two federal agents. All we want to do is talk to Ian DeRose and Jenna."

Dorian didn't move from where he stood beside Ray. "Well, I'm not as stupid as my friend Finn, so I don't tell my wife what to do."

"Take some notes, Bollinger," Charlie muttered from the other side of the room.

"Although, if Ray would let me," Dorian continued, "I would put myself between her and that weapon I know you have pointed at her under the table."

Ray shrugged with a little smile. "He's protective. But I'm protective of him too."

Callum shook his head. "We're not your enemy."

Ray's eyes narrowed. "The other people in this room, and maybe a dozen who aren't inside this building, are the people we know for a fact are not our enemies. Beyond those, I take no chances."

Callum brought his hands up from under the table and set his gun on the surface. "Not your enemy."

Dorian relaxed just the slightest bit now that a loaded gun wasn't pointed at his pregnant wife. Everyone did.

Until the door burst open behind Jenna. She spun and saw Ian and Mark rushing in, weapons raised. She forced herself to tear her eyes away from Mark and back to the booth. By then, both Callum and Craig had their guns in hand. At least both of them were smart enough not to point them at Ray, even though she had the crossbow.

Jenna held up a hand and put on her best Evelyn O'Connell from *The Mummy* voice. "Now, now, children. Let's all calm down. My brother isn't here to do anyone any harm. Callum may work with some people I find personally repulsive, but he's not a bad guy either."

She hoped that worked, because yelling *I am a librarian!* probably wouldn't make sense to anyone.

"We got word there was trouble," Ian said. "That Ray and Dorian had taken down some threats."

Ray shrugged and nodded toward the two men sitting across from her. "They were poking around. I don't like people who poke around when they've proven themselves untrustworthy once."

"They need to talk to you and me, Ian," Jenna said. "That's all they want."

Ian nodded and holstered his weapon. Slowly, everyone else did the same. Even Ray.

"You going to tell whoever you've got outside to stand down?" Mark said to Dorian.

It took Jenna a second to realize Mark was talking about some sort of sniper.

Dorian shrugged but then pulled out his phone and dialed a number. "We've got it handled. You can go. I owe you one. Thanks."

"Aiden?" Zac asked.

Dorian shook his head. "Gabe."

Callum's face went hard. "You had a former Navy SEAL like Gabriel Collingwood out there with his sights on us?"

Dorian leaned down onto the table so his face was close to the agents across from him. His voice was so soft Jenna could hardly hear his words.

"This woman and my children mean everything in the universe to me. Any threat, foreign or domestic, won't be tolerated. And believe me, Ray's insistence on hearing what you had to say is the only reason you're sitting here alive. Remember that next time you're thinking of sneaking into this town unannounced with an agenda. I have no problem hiding as many bodies as it takes to keep my family safe."

Ray stood, slipping her crossbow into the specialized

holster at her back. She kissed her husband on the cheek and grabbed his hand. "We're heading home. I need to get the lasagna in the oven."

Dorian let the tiny woman lead him out. As he passed by Jenna, he touched her on the shoulder. "Although burying those two would've made me a little sad on your account."

She winked at him. "Thanks for giving them a chance, Ghost."

Now that the crisis had passed, everyone in the bar began moving more normally. Ian went over to chew out Wavy's security detail. Finn picked up Charlie and hoisted her over his shoulder, carrying her out as she laughed. Zac followed behind them, offering a small salute as he left.

Jenna noticed Mark studying her but didn't say anything to him. Instead, she went and sat down across from her brother and Callum.

"You could've called," she said to Craig. "Easier than facing a crossbow."

Her brother gave a tight smile. "If Dorian knew what it felt like to be shot by that damned crossbow of hers, he would know I don't take it lightly."

Ian joined them and slid into the booth next to Jenna. "If I'm not mistaken, he's been on the receiving end of Ray's arrows before. Thing had a fucking note attached to it."

Craig looked over at the door Dorian and Ray had exited. "Those two are scary."

"Something you might want to keep in mind for future meetings." Mark took his place flanking Ian. Once again, Jenna avoided looking at him.

"Agreed," Ian said. "If you want an appointment with me, call my assistant."

Callum let out a sigh. "We needed both you and Jenna. After what happened with Theodore Wilson, I wasn't sure if Jenna would talk to me at all."

Jenna stiffened, and they all sat in silence at Wilson's name. The Europol agent had broken in to her house and used her agoraphobia against her a few months ago. His intentions may have been good, but his methods were still part of what was causing her to vomit after only a few seconds outside.

And worst of all, Mark Outlawson had been there to witness that entire showdown with Wilson.

"If Wilson is around, I'm sure I can call Ray and her crossbow back real quick," she finally said.

Callum shook his head. "No, he's in Europe where he belongs. This has nothing to do with him."

"Then what does it have to do with?" Mark's voice to her side was cold and hard, all hint of his normal Southern drawl completely gone.

Callum sat up straighter and looked at Jenna. "I asked Craig to come with me once we found out you were in Oak Creek. I was fairly certain you'd shut me down after what happened with Wilson, and I was hoping your brother might have more success in getting you to hear me out."

She met Craig's eyes. He hadn't said much, but that wasn't unusual for him. "Is this a case for you? I thought you were an analyst."

"I am. It's not my case. When Callum approached me, I told him I would help establish contact with you, but that I wouldn't try to talk you into it. What I say shouldn't have any bearing on your decision, sis."

"Although you should know—" Callum started.

"Shut up, Webb." Craig cut Callum off. "That's irrelevant."

She looked back and forth between the two men. "What's irrelevant?"

Craig shook his head. "Hear Callum out and decide if

you want to help. But only do it if you want to. You've already done enough."

That wasn't true. Craig might want to think so because he loved her and couldn't stand the thought of what she'd been through when she was held captive. But the truth was, Jenna could spend the rest of her life making up for the evil she'd helped create, and it still wouldn't be enough.

She turned to Callum. "What sort of assistance do you need?"

"We have an undercover agent who was killed."

She flinched but shook her head. "I'm sorry. Truly. But that's not my problem, and there are other people better equipped to help you." People who weren't regressing in their agoraphobia and weren't a half step from a breakdown.

There was a moment of silence as Callum geared up for his persuasive speech.

He didn't have to think it through too hard. She already knew what he was going to say. So she wasn't surprised at the words that came out of his mouth.

"The agent went undercover to gather intel about a human trafficking ring."

She knew what was coming. She knew and wished she could run so she didn't have to hear the rest of it. But where could she go? The only thing that scared her more than what Callum Webb was about to say was having to go outside to escape it.

"It's not a normal trafficking ring," Callum continued. "They're not using drugs or violence to control their victims. They're using chemical subjectification and gene editing."

Jenna could barely force air through her throat, it was so tightly closed to keep her scream from escaping.

"The traffickers are using the methods you created."

Chapter 5

Mark was putting an end to this right damned now. He didn't know if Ian and Craig couldn't see that Jenna was a half breath away from a total meltdown or didn't care.

"Enough," he said.

Callum met his eyes. "I'm not trying to be a bastard. Jenna is our best shot at stopping what's happening."

"How do you know it's from my projects?" Jenna whispered.

Projects. She said it like it was something she'd chosen to do at school, not that she'd been violently abducted and forced for months to do someone else's bidding.

Callum now looked at Ian. "We captured two people in the middle of crimes. Toxicology, blood work, and medical tests suggest genetic modifications and chemical subjectification."

Ian sat up straighter. "Like what was done to Wavy and Bronwyn Rourke."

Jenna got paler as Callum nodded. "Yes."

"That can't be right," Ian said. "We took out Mosaic.

Disbanded them completely. There's no way they're still in the human trafficking business."

Mark placed a hand on Ian's shoulder in support. Even thinking about what had happened to his wife still tore Ian up, despite Wavy making an almost complete recovery. Former Zodiac agent Bronwyn Rourke had been subjected to similar abuse by Mosaic and would wear the mental scars from her ordeal for the rest of her life.

Saying Mosaic—a pretty word for an ugly group of terrorists—was back in operation was akin to telling Ian he'd be going back to the front line of a particularly brutal war.

"No, not Mosaic," Callum replied. "But it's another group using similar methods."

Ian relaxed slightly, but Jenna didn't. "What do you want from me?" she asked. "I can't go out into the field."

"Nobody—at least no good guys—know this research better than you." Mark caught Jenna's flinch. Callum hadn't meant to, but he'd just lumped her in with the criminals. "We need you to look at the data—medical tests, autopsy reports—and tell us what we're missing. Tell us how we can stop what's happening. The data can be sent to you for you to work remotely."

"You don't have to do this," Craig told his sister when Jenna didn't respond.

Callum narrowed his eyes. "You should also know—"

"Shut up, Webb," Craig said again.

"—that as thanks for your assistance, your brother would be reinstated as an active FBI agent. He'd no longer be relegated to data analysis."

Jenna's eyes flew to Craig's. "Is this true?"

He leaned forward. "What it is, is irrelevant. I'm happy in my job as an analyst. I'm doing good work there. Important work. I won't let them blackmail you into doing something you don't want to do."

All information now on the table, everyone looked at one another for a long moment.

"I'll do it." Jenna's voice was much calmer than Mark expected.

Craig shook his head. "Jenna, you don't—"

She held up a hand to stop her brother. "No, I'll do it. You getting reinstated as an active agent is a bonus. I helped make this mess. I need to help clean it up."

"Thank you," Callum said. "Your expertise will make a huge difference. The terrorist group we're up against—"

She held up her hand once more. "No offense, but I don't want to know. The last time your *team* needed my help they didn't give a shit about what it cost me."

Callum grimaced. "You're talking about what happened with Agent Wilson."

Callum continued when Jenna didn't respond. "Look, Wilson went off on his own with that stunt. I would never condone the measures he used to—"

Mark clenched his hands into fists. He'd been there for what had happened with Wilson. He'd seen how much it had cost Jenna.

"I don't care if you condoned it or not," Jenna said. "I'll look through the intel you provide and give you my report on the physical findings. But beyond that, I want nothing to do with you or the case." She turned to Ian. "Excuse me, I need out of this booth."

Ian got up so she could slide out, and Jenna walked to the other side of the bar.

"She's tying all our hands by refusing to look at the big picture," Callum muttered.

"You got what you want, Webb, so count your blessings." Craig stood up. "I'm going to talk with my sister."

Ian slid over so Mark could sit beside him. They both

looked over at Callum. He was a good guy, but right now, that wasn't evident.

"Craig is right," Ian said. "Even only focusing on some of the intel, Jenna will provide you more assistance than most people could with every bit of the information."

"If you say so." Callum rubbed his eyes. "It seems like she's overreacting. I know she has trauma from her captivity and doesn't like to be around other people or go outside. But it's not like Wilson dragged her out of her house at gunpoint."

Mark glared at the man. "I saw it. You didn't. That fucker Wilson did a lot of damage, even if it wasn't physical."

Ian nodded. "Jenna hasn't been actively working for Zodiac since then. She wanted extended leave."

Callum leaned against the back of the booth. He looked exhausted. "Look, I'm not trying to be the resident asshole. I don't want to see anyone traumatized, but we need help. People are dying. I came to you because I knew you were invested because of what happened with Wavy and Bronwyn. I thought Jenna would be too."

Mark looked over at where Jenna was talking to Craig. Her features were still pinched and pale. "She is invested. But her involvement comes at a high price. Nobody should forget that."

"Tell us what you know about the traffickers," Ian demanded.

Callum wiped a hand down his face. "The agent who was killed was undercover in Joaquin Martinez's organization."

Both Mark and Ian sat up straighter. Joaquin Martinez— he and his organization generally known as just *Joaquin*—was definitely as ruthless as Mosaic had been. Perhaps his organi-

zation wasn't as big, but he was smart, efficient, and brutal—
an ugly combination.

"We have intel thanks to the micro transmitter Zodiac
was able to place on him at that wedding in the islands last
year. But he discovered it and our agent a few days ago.
Transmitter and agent came back to us in pieces."

"Shit," Ian muttered.

Zodiac had been happy to help with the undercover
mission, but damn, it sucked it had resulted in someone's
death.

"Before we lost our guy, we got word about Joaquin's
latest venture—a genetics research lab. Human subjects
being brainwashed through chemical subjectification and
gene editing and then being controlled by him."

Ian bit out a curse. That was exactly what had happened
when Zodiac Tactical had been battling Mosaic.

Mark scrubbed a hand down his face. "What is he using
them for?"

"The two we know about so far were both used for theft.
One—white male, twenty-three years old—broke in to a
jewelry store in Sacramento. One—black female, twenty
years old—hit a pawn shop in Dallas. Both killed themselves
when they were about to be taken into custody."

That wasn't what Mark had been expecting. "Killing
themselves seems like overkill for a break-in."

Callum nodded. "Our undercover man was able to get us
enough intel that we knew they were both victims of the
brainwashing—postmortem   blood   and   tox   reports
confirmed. I'm not sure we would've ever linked the two
together otherwise."

Out of the corner of his eye, Mark saw Jenna and Craig
stand up from their table and hug each other. He thought
they both would leave, but Jenna walked him to the door,

and then, with one more hug, turned back and sat down alone at the table.

"What do you need from us?" Ian asked. "Zodiac will help stop this sort of mind-control bullshit in any way we can. Like you said, I'm invested."

Ian smiled over at his wife on the other side of the bar, and Callum and Mark looked over too. She waved at him and hooked her thumb toward some of the Linear Tactical gang who were getting ready to leave, obviously signifying she was going with them.

The love between Ian and Wavy was damned near palpable.

Ian wasn't lying when he said he was invested. Mark knew he would use any and all of his considerable fortune to stop Joaquin. Not to mention his resources from owning Zodiac Tactical, one of the most well-respected security businesses in the world.

Mark would be right there by his side when Ian did it.

"Mostly, I needed to get in touch with you to get to Jenna. She's not exactly taking my calls these days. I thought coming here to Oak Creek would be the least painful way to talk with her."

Mark couldn't help but grin. "How's that working out for you?"

"I don't currently have a crossbow bolt projecting from my body, so I'll call it a win." Callum rolled his eyes. "But we need Jenna's help. Without it, we're going to remain two steps behind Joaquin, and people are going to keep dying."

Mark glanced over at her, and Ian and Callum continued to talk about details. She'd ordered some food, and the Eagle's Nest owner Lexi had brought it over. Jenna still looked stressed even when she smiled at Lexi and began to eat.

Just once, Mark would like to see Jenna *not* looking that way. He'd like to see her smiling, relaxed, tousled.

He'd like to be a part of making her all three.

He turned his attention back to the conversation. Whatever he wanted with Jenna would have to wait. First, he needed to help stop a killer.

Chapter 6

Jenna was running out of excuses to stay at the Eagle's Nest. Craig had left thirty minutes ago, needing to get back to his job.

It had been good to see her brother. Jenna was well aware that she was the cause for the distance between them. He'd sacrificed a lot to get her out of captivity, and she truly was thankful. But she'd kept him at arm's length, not willing to let him know how much of a mental mess she was.

Craig was torn about her agreeing to help Callum. Honestly, so was she. When Callum offered to help have Craig reinstated as an active agent, that had definitely tipped the scales in his favor. But she would've helped either way.

What choice did she have? The traffickers using the chemical subjectification and gene editing may have been the monsters, but Jenna was the Dr. Frankenstein who had given them their powers. If she could take the powers away, it was her responsibility to do that. She should already be back home digging into the particulars of the case.

But someone had moved her car away from the front door.

It was her own fault. She'd been such a train wreck when she'd arrived at the Eagle's Nest she'd left the keys in it and the security system turned off. Someone had thought they were doing her a favor and moved it to the parking lot.

Maybe Lexi wouldn't notice if Jenna decided to live here forever.

Every time she tried to work up the nerve to head for the door, she was swallowed by panic. The first time, she'd sat back down and ordered a soda. The next time, she'd ordered some food. The third time, she'd claimed to need a cup of coffee.

She was running out of excuses and only had a half cup of coffee left.

"Mind if I join you?"

Mark Outlawson slid into the booth across from her without waiting for a reply.

She raised an eyebrow. "What if I say no, you can't join me?"

He raised an eyebrow of his own over those striking green eyes. "Then I'll point out that I know you're still here because you're afraid to walk out to your car."

She broke eye contact to make sure no one else was in hearing distance. It was midafternoon, and now that the drama had passed, everyone had gone home. Callum and Ian had just left together.

Except for the two of them, and Lexi over by the bar, the Eagle's Nest was empty. No one could hear their conversation.

That didn't mean Jenna wanted to continue it. "I don't know what you're talking about."

"We *both* know what I'm talking about."

"I'll admit today was a little exciting and I'd already had a little stress at home." Damn it, why had she said that? "I'm decompressing with a meal and coffee. Doesn't mean I'm afraid to walk to my car."

"Did the stress at home have something to do with your bruised knuckles?"

Her hands were under the table. How did he know about them?

"I saw them when you were talking to Callum," Mark continued when she didn't answer.

"It was from a workout. I sometimes do a little…martial arts for exercise." She brought them up and laid them on the table near her coffee cup.

He reached out and took one hand gently, rubbing his thumb across her knuckles. "Hitting things can be a good way to relieve stress. What sort of martial arts do you study?"

She should pull her hand away; she knew she should. And yet…she didn't. She liked to be touched. Moreover… she liked to be touched by *this* man.

"No one specific style. It's sort of a hodgepodge."

She'd been less interested in mastering one style and more interested in making sure she was as deadly as she could be.

Of course, that had come back to bite her in the ass too. Which was why letting him touch her was a mistake. She slipped her hand away from his and wrapped it around her mug.

"Thanks for stopping by to check on me. I'll be fine. I'm leaving as soon as I finish this coffee."

Lexi chose that moment to walk over. "Need a warm-up?"

"No, I'm good."

The former movie star smiled. "Well, your meal and coffee are on me since you rushed out here and saved me from needing to mop up blood. But if you stay much longer, I might have to start charging you rent."

Jenna forced a smile. "Yeah, don't worry, I'm getting out of here. Thanks for the meal."

Lexi smiled back. "Good to see you in town. I know you don't get out much. You're welcome any time. Both of you."

Lexi left to go take an order from another customer who'd walked in. Mark was making no move to leave. He'd leaned back and put his arm along the booth.

He was studying her with those intense green eyes. It was all she could do not to squirm.

"Everyone here thinks you choose not to get out much. They don't know the truth."

What was she supposed to say to that? Explain that she'd been *regressing* since she'd been rescued from captivity eighteen months ago? That she was getting worse, not better?

She crossed her arms over her chest. "Believe it or not, I don't discuss my personal life with most people. I have a lot of friends in Oak Creek, but I don't want to burden them."

"If they're your friends, then the truth wouldn't be a burden. They'll want to help you."

She took the last sip of her coffee then slid the cup toward the end of the table. "Well, there's not much they can do, so there's no point in my making a whole production out of it. And I'd appreciate it if you'd do the same. Everyone knows I don't like to go out. That's close enough to the truth."

One of his eyebrows rose again. "Except for times like right now where you're basically trapped in a building. If your friends knew what was going on, they could help you."

"You think you know me so well, *Outlaw*?" She used his Zodiac code name like it was some creative insult, when all it was was an accurate description of his sexy personality. "Just because you happened to witness that asshole Theodore Wilson get the drop on me? You don't know shit."

She was overreacting. They both knew it, but he remained calm, which just pissed her off more.

"He used your weaknesses against you. That can happen to anybody."

They stared at each other, that day a few months ago resting between them. Mark didn't say anything.

Was he remembering her curled up on the floor, begging Wilson not to take her outside like he threatened to?

Was he remembering having to carry her to her bed once Wilson left and give her a sedative because she couldn't get herself under control?

Was he remembering how weak and pathetic she'd been?

Thank God he didn't know that she'd gotten even worse since then.

Mark reached for her hands on the table, but she slid them back. "I'm not trying to act like I know you. Although I would like to get to know you better if you'd let me. You know that."

She did know that. He'd made multiple attempts to talk to her in the past few months. It was one of the reasons she'd run and hidden in Oak Creek.

She stood up. "I don't think that's a good idea. I've got a lot of work to do, and I'm not looking for any new friends."

She winced. She was being such a bitch. But he already knew too much truth about her. Truth she was desperate to keep everyone else from knowing.

And even with all the truth he did know, he didn't know everything. Didn't know the most important parts.

And he never would. No one would.

"See you around, Outlaw."

He didn't say a word as she walked away. But as she got to the door, her steps slowed like she was sludging through mire. Every step got heavier and harder to take.

Through the glass, she could see her car parked in the lot

fifty feet away. It might as well have been fifty miles. She couldn't make it. She froze a few feet from the door.

No.

No, she could not panic now. She had to walk outside to her car. She refused to make a fool out of herself here. In front of Mark, in front of Lexi. Word would get around to everyone.

But she couldn't force herself to move. She demanded her arm reach for the door handle, but it stayed pinned to her side. She couldn't move forward, couldn't even move backward.

She could feel sweat already pooling on her forehead. The sounds from the bar became muffled around her. It was like she was outside her own body.

There was no brute-forcing her way through these panic attacks. Multiple therapists had warned her of that. People who didn't experience them often thought someone could *mind-over-matter* them. Think happy thoughts and the panic would recede.

That wasn't true. All she could do was survive.

She felt someone behind her, and a deep voice whispered in her ear. "I'm going to pull your car up to the door."

Mark.

His voice pulled her back from the dread spinning through her mind like a cyclone. She looked over at him. He had bent his legs so their faces were on the same level. All she could see were those green eyes.

"I—I—" She couldn't get further words out.

"I know," he whispered. "Stay here. Let me get the car."

"Hey, you okay, Jenna?" Lexi called from behind her.

She couldn't answer. Thankfully, Mark answered for her. "I think our girl's had a stressful day. I'm going to drive her home. Let me grab her car and bring it up to the door."

"You Zodiac guys are such gentlemen," Lexi responded. "Of course, my hubby is too."

Mark got right in front of Jenna's face again. "I'm going outside and getting the car. Stay here."

As if she could go anywhere else. Before she could say a word, he was gone. She watched, still feeling outside her own body, as he ran to get her car then pulled it just as close as she had when she'd arrived. A few seconds later, he was back at her side.

"I'm going to put my arm around you, and we'll make a dash for it. Okay?"

She forced words out. "I can drive."

He rolled those green eyes. "There's no way in hell I'm letting you drive. I'll get you home then call Ian to come get me."

She wanted to argue, but she didn't have it in her.

And then his arm was around her, and they were moving. She didn't even have a chance to take a breath or freak out more—they were outside.

And just as the fear began to claw her from the inside out, he opened the passenger's side door and she was in the car.

She was safe.

She could breathe.

She snapped back into her own body.

Mark ran around and got in behind the wheel. She didn't try to talk, just pressed the navigation button on the console so he'd know where to go.

He didn't talk on the way either, which was good since she wasn't sure she could answer. At a red light, he shot off a text with her address.

As they pulled up to her house, she pressed in the code for her garage, and he pulled the car all the way inside and shut it off. She still didn't say anything.

"I'll get out then you close the garage door behind me."

She nodded. She wanted to say more—to say thanks or laugh this off in some way, but she couldn't. She'd been stretched too thin too many times today.

"Get some rest. Put ice on those knuckles, or they'll hurt even worse tomorrow."

With that, he was gone. As soon as he made it out of the garage, she closed the door behind him.

And cried for the second time that day.

Chapter 7

"We have another dead body."

Mark looked up from the plans he was drawing in the Linear Tactical conference room. He didn't often put his architectural and civil engineering background to much use, even though the Navy had made sure he had ample experience in both. But he had been for the past few days since Callum had shown up at the Eagle's Nest.

And now here he was, back again.

Mark set his pencil behind his ear. "I assume you let Ray and Dorian know you were coming to Oak Creek this time since you're not the dead body in question."

Callum rolled his eyes. "Yes, I did, even though as actual law enforcement, that shouldn't be required."

"They're protective of this town."

Callum leaned one shoulder against the doorframe. "I suppose it's nice for Oak Creek to have its own set of highly trained watch dogs. Even though neither of them actually exists in any database."

Mark folded his arms over his chest. "That's not a string I'd pull on too hard."

Despite being the one to train them, the US government had turned its back on Dorian and Ray—Ray, especially—and labeled them enemies to the republic.

Ray and Dorian had come through hell to create a new life for themselves. Nobody in Oak Creek was going to let that be lost.

"I'm not. The Lindstroms are not my concern, neither now nor in the future. I have real bad guys to fight."

Fair enough. "So, another dead body. What happened?"

"Third victim, broke in to a jewelry show in Dallas. This one didn't die quickly. White male, nineteen years old."

"He didn't kill himself when he was arrested like the others?"

"No, law enforcement stopped him. But he went into some sort of cardiac failure while in holding. They got him to the hospital, but he continued to deteriorate from there. Died a few hours later. Nothing the doctors did to stop it helped."

Mark gritted his teeth. "You can bet your ass Joaquin was behind that too."

"Undoubtedly. This was some sort of fail-safe. We assume to keep the robots from spilling information about him and his organization. They have some sort of chemical in their system or something."

"That one was basically a kid. Nineteen years old?"

Callum rubbed a hand over his dark hair. "They're all basically kids. Besides the fact that they're young, so far, we can't find any tie between the robots or the places they've broken in to. All we know is that they're programmed to die rather than let law enforcement interrogate them."

Mark gripped the table. "That basically makes Joaquin a serial killer, just in a slightly more unique way."

Callum nodded. "My feelings exactly. That's why I'm going undercover."

"Are you sure that's a good idea? Joaquin's got to be on high guard after the last agent was discovered."

"It's a risk, but I've got an in, so I'm going to take it."

Mark understood. If it meant Callum might be able to stop these robots and save lives, it would be worth the risk. Callum was a good agent.

"What do you need from me?" There was a reason Callum was here. "Ian's already gone back to New York."

"I know. He let me know you were still here. I need you to take point on this side of things."

Mark raised an eyebrow. He'd stayed in Oak Creek because Linear Tactical had needed help on some general building repairs. Then as he'd started talking to Zac Mackay about some expansions they planned to make—service and emotional support animal training like their friends at the Resting Warrior Ranch in Montana—Mark had agreed to help draw up some of that.

And of course, Mark had wanted to stick close to Oak Creek in case he could help Jenna out with this case. He hadn't seen her in the three days since pulling her car into her garage.

Hadn't been able to get the look of despair that had blanketed her features out of his mind.

"What do you need me to do?"

"I have files that need to be delivered to Jenna. I know she's an extreme introvert, so I didn't want to just knock on her door. I was afraid she might have a crossbow too."

Mark laughed, but he shook his head. The more time he had spent around Jenna, the more he realized that most of her colleagues, like Callum, generally assumed her desire not to go outside was based on not wanting to be around people. The assumption made sense. She was a computer whiz—the type of person often known for their introversion—plus her time in captivity helped explain her aversion to being surrounded by people.

But that wasn't the case. Mark had been around her enough to see that Jenna definitely didn't want to go outside, but it wasn't because she didn't want to be around people. Getting her out of the Eagle's Nest the other day had proven it. She hadn't been uncomfortable at all talking to everyone in the bar.

She wasn't quiet and reserved—shying away from people.

But she'd been absolutely terrified to go from the building to her car.

He'd been prepared to help her through the drive home, but she hadn't needed it. She'd been relatively fine once she'd made it inside the vehicle.

It was only outside that terrified Jenna. *The outdoors.*

Most people who suffered from agoraphobia avoided crowded places that might make them feel trapped—usually buildings or public transport. Jenna's seemed to be triggered by being outside.

Mark had no idea why that was the case. And it seemed most of her friends and colleagues weren't aware of it at all. They just assumed she wanted to stay in her house—alone.

Jenna was a fucking expert when it came to holding people at arm's length. She'd spun an *I'm-an-introvert-leave-me-alone* narrative around herself, and everyone had bought it like it was a best seller.

"So, you think she'll be more receptive to me bringing the info over?" Mark asked. "Maybe I need to be scared of crossbows also."

Callum shrugged. "You two seemed pretty friendly sitting in the booth when I left the Eagle's Nest the other day. Maybe she'll open the door for you. Or at least not shoot you first."

"Fine." Mark put his pencil back down on the table. The building plans he'd been working on for Linear Tactical's expansion would have to wait.

"I need you as more than just a glorified messenger. We discovered that Joaquin had connections to Adil Garrison before Garrison was arrested."

"The fallen billionaire?"

Callum nodded. "The fallen billionaire who held Jenna captive for eighteen months."

Shit. "Joaquin and Garrison knew each other?"

"We're almost positive that's how Joaquin is able to use the chemical subjectification and gene editing. He got the info from Garrison."

Mark rubbed the back of his neck. "Which means Joaquin might know about Jenna's existence."

"I know she doesn't want to hear the details outside of the part she is specifically working on, but she might be in danger. That's why I'm here in person. Despite Jenna thinking I'm an asshole, I really don't want anything to happen to her."

"Believe me, I'm not going to let it." Mark didn't care if he had to sleep every night outside her house in his car.

"Ian says he's sending help for Jenna, but he was vague about the specifics. Taking Joaquin down before he can perfect his control over the robots is of critical importance to Ian."

"Because it almost happened to his wife and his best friend's wife. It's personal for him."

Callum let out a hard breath. "I don't want anyone else to die. I want to stop this bastard. Joaquin is up to something big, I can feel it. What we've experienced so far is just the tip of the iceberg. I've got to stop him."

Mark reached over and shook his hand. "Be careful

undercover. You can trust I'll take care of things on this end while you're gone."

No one was getting to Jenna on his watch.

An hour later, Mark was sitting outside Jenna's house. He hadn't paid too much attention to it a few days ago when driving her home.

The house looked somewhat similar to many of the homes in the area. There were no near neighbors—a popular Wyoming trait. It was small—one story, with a bonus room over the garage. It was built on a slight hill, with a porch that would provide nice views of the nearby Tetons.

Most people would've immediately put a swing or chairs out on that porch, but Jenna hadn't. If Mark's hunch was correct, she probably hadn't been out there at all.

If she disliked the outdoors so much, he wasn't sure why she'd bought a house here at all, but evidently, she'd owned it for nearly a year. According to Zac, she hadn't told anyone in town when she bought it and hadn't spent much time at it.

Or if she had, she hadn't told any of her Oak Creek friends she was there, seeing as how she was so *introverted* and all.

The narrative Jenna was determined to spin.

As Mark got out of the car, files in hand, he noticed some of the details of the house he'd missed before. Cameras covering all angles of the property. Two that were automatically following him as he moved.

No one was going to sneak up on Jenna unawares.

He gave one of the cameras a little wave and walked up to the door. He didn't bother knocking. She knew he was there.

Sure enough, a few seconds later, a voice came out of a speaker over the doorbell. "Go away, Outlaw."

He held up the files. He didn't see a camera here at the door, but he had no doubt there was one. "Callum sent me. I have more intel on the robots. There's been another case."

"Why didn't he just send them to me electronically?"

"He wanted to talk to me in person. He's going undercover. Want to let me in, and we can discuss it not through a door, little librarian?"

There was silence for a moment. "Why did you just call me that?"

"Look, you may not be an explorer or an adventurer or a treasure-seeker, but you're proud of what you are."

"And what is that?"

He grinned. Good. She got *The Mummy* reference. He thought that was what she'd been semi-quoting the other day at the Eagle's Nest, but he hadn't been sure.

"You…are *a librarian*," he said.

"Technically, you're supposed to pass out drunk as you say that, if you're going to be completely accurate to the film."

He could hear the smile in her voice. He chuckled. "Let me in, librarian."

She opened the door, her body as far away from the outside as it could be while her hand still held the knob. That confirmed his suspicions about her disliking the outdoors.

He walked in quickly, and she shut the door behind him, leaning heavily against it. Her hair was up in a ponytail with tendrils falling around her flushed face. She'd been in the middle of some sort of exercise.

When he'd first met Jenna—on a computer screen for a Zodiac mission—she'd had black hair. Later, she'd dyed it blond. Neither of those had ever seemed quite right. Now, her hair had grown out and was a light, sun-kissed brown. This was probably her natural color.

Most of the times he'd seen her over the computer

screen, she'd been wearing glasses, but not now. Now, those big brown eyes—honey-colored—were staring up at him.

"There's another robot?" she asked.

"Yeah. I don't know that I like that we're calling them that. These are human beings."

She shook her head. "I don't call them that to strip them of their humanity. They're being forced to do as they are programmed. The robot is a part of them that they can't control. They can't be held responsible for their choices. We have to find a way to separate the robot from the person."

Fair enough. "This one didn't survive either. He didn't kill himself upon capture, but his system started shutting down, and he died a few hours later."

Those brown eyes narrowed, and she pushed away from the door. Mark followed her as she walked farther into the house.

"That means they're leaving tails in the robots."

"Tails?"

She led him into the kitchen then grabbed a bottle of water from the fridge. She handed him one too. "It's part of the regimen I helped create. Leaving a tail in chemical subjectification means that without the given chemicals, the person's body will start attacking itself. Did this newest robot have a heart attack?"

He nodded. "Yes, cardiac arrest is how he finally died. The other info is in these files."

She slumped back against the refrigerator. "This is my fault."

"You know it's not. No matter what you may have initially created while you were held captive, this is not your fault."

She shook her head. Mark was going to argue further, but she pulled out the files and set them on the kitchen island and began looking through them.

"Jenna, there's more."

She looked at him. "More dead bodies?"

"I know you didn't want any details beyond what you're working on, but Callum found ties between Joaquin Martinez and—"

"Adil Garrison," she finished for him.

"Yes. How did you know?"

"I figured that out after looking at the details of the first two robots. The chemicals and gene work done on the two of them wasn't just similar to what I developed, it was exactly the same regimen."

"I'm sorry," Mark said. "But if Joaquin was connected to Garrison and is using your regimen, he has to know you exist. You could be in danger."

Chapter 8

Mark was getting too old for this sleeping in the car shit. He'd done it enough in his years working as a bodyguard to know the trade secrets: best types of food and drinks to have, the ways of keeping yourself awake and focused in the deepest hours of the night, how to clench and release different muscle groups so he'd be ready to move without stiffness if the situation arose.

But it all still sucked.

At least his peripheral neuropathy wasn't acting up. That was both the good and bad part about the condition—it could go weeks or months at a time without flare-ups. He never knew when it was going to hit him. It was forcing him to learn to live a day at a time.

It was just before midnight when he got a text from Jenna.

Stop being Creeper McCreepy and come sleep on the couch.

He had to laugh at that. The woman was definitely not quiet and reserved.

Mark had never gone for quiet and reserved.

He grabbed his gear and headed back toward her house.

Jenna had been surprisingly calm at hearing about the link between Joaquin and Adil Garrison. Granted, Garrison was serving life in prison without the possibility of parole, so he couldn't hurt her. But Mark had expected more of a reaction from her.

She may be confident there was no danger, but until they knew for sure Joaquin wasn't targeting her, Mark would be on her like glue.

Not that that was any sort of hardship.

As he got to the front door, she again opened it, staying back from the outside. Once he was in, she reengaged the multiple locks on the doors.

"Same locks as your house in Denver?" he asked.

She shrugged one small shoulder. "I actually got a little lazy in my Denver house. Too complacent. That's how Wilson was able to pull his little stunt. I'm taking measures to rectify that."

Mark winced. "I'm the one who led Wilson to you. That's on me. I'm sorry."

He would never forget the sight of her curled into a ball on the floor, completely helpless, terrified of being taken into custody by the Europol agent.

"He was determined to find Bronwyn and me eventually, so don't blame yourself. It was an important lesson for me. Like I said, I'd become too complacent."

He tilted his head to the side. "You've upped security at your house there?"

"There. Here. All of them."

"All? How many houses do you have?"

She crossed her arms over her chest. "Six."

"Holy shit. Why do you need six houses?"

She walked past him and motioned for him to follow, leading him back to her living room. A pillow and folded blanket were already on the couch. "I like to have options."

"In case you need to go to ground?"

She didn't deny it. "Yes. I'm sure you have more than one ID you can use if you need it, right? It's sort of the same principle."

He tossed his bag on the floor by the couch. "No. Actually, Mark Outlawson is my only alias. I'm not a spy. I don't plan to need to disappear suddenly."

She narrowed her eyes. "We might need to rectify that. I could do it for you pretty easily if you just wanted a basic package. I've created personas and backgrounds for Ray and Dorian and their kids. If they needed to disappear, they could do so in an instant."

"I wouldn't be surprised if Ray and Dorian had more than one alias."

"Absolutely. Probably two or three more handled by other computer experts. Gives them options if needed."

Mark sat down on the couch. "Is doing stuff like that how you afford all your houses?"

Jenna was a genius on multiple different levels—she had advanced degrees in both bioengineering and computer science. No doubt, that genius was why she'd been kidnapped by Adil Garrison.

With Zodiac, at least Mark knew she was working on the side of the angels. But what she did on her own time might not be so innocent.

She tilted her head to the side and studied him. "Don't tell me someone with a code name of *Outlaw* has a problem with my creating alternate IDs for a family who has done a lot to help a lot of people."

"I don't have a problem with you creating them for the Lindstroms. I'm just wondering if you do the same for others who might not be quite as savory."

"Don't worry, Boy Scout. IDs are not my specialty, so I don't do that sort of work often."

"But you do some sort of work to afford six different safe houses."

Mark grimaced. Maybe he shouldn't press. He wasn't sure if he wanted to know.

She leaned against the doorframe, relaxed and comfortable here in her own home. "I do. But don't worry, nothing illegal. I'm on a monthly retainer for over a dozen Fortune 500 companies. They hire me to make regular attempts to get through their firewalls and tell them how they can improve cybersecurity. It pays very well—seven-figure well."

"Then why do you work for Zodiac?"

"Because I want to stop people like Joaquin. Because I want to help people and make up for the damage I've done."

He wanted to tell her that she couldn't hold herself responsible for what she'd been forced to create when her life was in jeopardy. But he knew those words were much easier for him to say than for her to accept.

He nodded. "We'll work together to stop Joaquin. Between us and Callum being undercover, we'll make sure this all stops and Joaquin goes down."

"I hope so." She looked smaller. More fragile.

He wanted to walk over and pull her into his arms. Wanted to do a hell of a lot more than just that, but right now, he would be more than content with merely holding her.

But she was already closing herself off from him. She pushed off from the doorway. "You're in for the night, right? Won't be going back outside?"

"Not planning on it."

"If you do need to go outside for any reason, wake me up first. Once I put the nighttime security measures in place, this house is pretty...locked down. You'll hurt yourself trying to get out with it on secure mode."

He raised an eyebrow. "What sort of *hurt myself* are we talking about?"

"Inside, you're fine. But if you open a door or window to the outside, you're going to find the kind of *hurt yourself* that would give Indiana Jones a run for his money."

He had to smile at that. "Giant boulders and poisonous darts?"

"Yep. Also, lasers that will burn straight through your skin and motion-activated firearms."

Shit. She wasn't kidding. "Great. I'll just pray you don't have an aneurysm in your sleep. If so, I'll stuff your body in the freezer and live out the rest of my days here in your house."

She cracked a smile at that one. "If there's an emergency, the temporary shutdown code is 542727426. That will buy you a one-minute shutdown of the weapons system."

He rolled his eyes. "Yeah, I'm sure I'll remember that, no problem."

She smiled. "If you have trouble, it's the numbers that spell out…*librarian*."

Jenna worked well into the night—Mark heard her clacking away on her computer from his place on the couch. But his time in the military had taught him to sleep whenever and however he could. He dozed off to the sound.

When he woke just after dawn, she'd gone to bed. Hoping what she'd said about inside being safe from all her booby traps was true, he got up, folded the blanket, and padded toward the kitchen to make himself some coffee.

Then he decided to have a look around. It didn't take him long to realize the unassuming appearance of the house on the outside was the exact opposite of what Jenna's house actually was on the inside.

For one, it was much larger than it appeared from outside. Whoever had designed this for her had cleverly utilized the hill the house sat on and had built into that slope. That made the inside square footage of the home more than double what it looked like from the exterior.

And she'd used most of that extra square footage for a gym and sparring area.

He worked on a daily basis with men and women who kept in top physical form—a requirement for a company like Zodiac. Jenna's gym would give some of their workout places a run for their money.

Strength equipment, free weights, and all sorts of sparring paraphernalia—which would explain the bruises on her knuckles at the Eagle's Nest. Evidently, she took her workouts and martial arts training very seriously.

How had he not known that about her? Not that Jenna shared much about herself with anyone. But this was another piece of her puzzle.

He finished his exploring, staying out of the room with the closed door that he assumed was her bedroom, then changed into workout clothes and headed back to her gym.

Today was a good day for his body. No muscle weakness or cramps in his legs or arms. He did a few rounds of weights then used her dummies for sparring.

By the time he was finished, he was covered in sweat and found Jenna watching from the doorway.

"You didn't get much sleep." He grabbed a small towel from the folded pile in the corner and wiped sweat off his face.

She had her own coffee cup in hand. "I'm not a big sleeper. Never really have been, then after my captivity, sleep got even harder."

There had been times like that for him also. His years in the Special Forces had given him enough fodder for more than one nightmare.

"I hope you don't mind me making use of this great space."

She smiled, a genuine one that almost took his breath away. "Not at all. I spend a crap-ton of time down here."

"The architectural design of this house is impressive. I'm sure you know that from the outside, it looks much smaller than it really is."

"Yeah, that was deliberate."

"Did you design it?"

"No way. That sort of design is not in my wheelhouse. But I definitely love this space."

"Your designer did a good job. It's very clever."

Her smile got bigger. "I'll have to show you the safe room and weapon storage spaces she added. Not to mention the materials that were used to do the upgrades. Looks like regular house stuff but is much stronger—bullet- and explosives-proof in a lot of places."

She was relaxed here because she felt safe. He liked to see it on her.

"A lot of people wouldn't have realized the difference between the outside and inside. Are you into architecture?" she asked.

"Yeah. Actually, I got a lot of training in civil and architectural engineering when I was in the military. So I definitely appreciate good and clever design when I see it."

Jenna's eyebrows rose in surprise. "Really? An engineer?"

"Yep. I know it doesn't exactly match up with most people's views about me, or probably any former Special Forces soldier."

"No," she said. "It wouldn't have been what I expected."

He saw the opportunity and took it. "Kind of like how

none of your friends have any idea you're struggling because you hide it so well?"

Immediately, her face turned cold. "Mark, stop. Please."

"All right. I just don't like to see you struggle. Do you think your friends—these friends—would judge you for what you've been through? We've all been through something."

"I know that." Her voice was even, but her knuckles were white gripping her coffee mug. "But what I share is my choice. Okay?"

He shouldn't have pushed. He held his hands out in a gesture of surrender. "Got it. Want to show me what you've been working on with the case?"

She relaxed slightly. "Sure. But I'll warn you, it's not exciting."

Grabbing his water bottle, he followed. He was in desperate need of a shower now, but he wasn't going to protest. At least she hadn't shut down completely.

He followed her into the office and watched her fold herself into the chair in front of her setup like she was made to be there. This was her true safe space. Here, she was in control and held all the power. He liked seeing the subtle straightening of her shoulders and the easing of her muscles. Relaxation and confidence looked damn good on Jenna Franklin.

She brought up pictures of all three robots on to the main screen. "Basically, I've got nothing. I've confirmed it's my original formula they're using to control the robots, but that's about it. I haven't found anything to connect the three victims, nor the locations they broke in to."

"It's early. You just got the info about the third robot last night."

"People are dying." Her voice was tight. "And it's my methodology that is causing it. I said I would help, but I'm useless."

He resisted the urge to step closer to her and offer comfort. "You offered to help," he said gently. "Whatever you can contribute fulfills that bargain. Your eyes on this data are worth a hundred people who don't know what's going on here. No one is expecting you to crack this on your own."

"Yeah." She didn't sound convinced.

They stood in silence for a moment before Jenna looked at him. "This may take more than a couple days. Am I going to find you sleeping in your car again?"

"Yes." He would. Didn't matter how long this took.

"Remember what I said about laser beams and automated guns? I'll be fine."

Her security system was top-notch, and there was every chance she would be okay. But the sight of her pleading on the floor a few months ago was still vivid in his mind, and he wouldn't be able to live with himself if something did happen to her and he wasn't there to stop it.

He knew she wasn't his to protect, even if he wished she were. But there was something here he couldn't walk away from. Jenna needed help, and he needed to help her.

"I'm sticking around here, no matter the booby traps you've got planned for anyone who comes after you. But I have plenty of experience at surveillance from inside my car. I'll be fine."

Those honey eyes studied him. After a minute, she stood. "Follow me."

He did, surprised when she didn't lead him to the front door. Instead, she led him to the other end of the house, where there was a room with a bed.

"Guest room for as long as you need it. The same security rules apply. You know the emergency code, but if you need to come in or leave, let me know. It would be a pity to have you flattened by my rolling boulder."

"As long as you're not spraying salt acid at me for trying to unearth an ancient curse, I think we'll be fine."

He caught her smile as she stepped out into the hall and grabbed some towels from a closet and handed them to him. "No salt acid. I keep that for the real bad guys."

"Thank you."

"You can stay until this is over," she said. "That's it, Outlaw."

He couldn't stop his smile. "You got it."

Chapter 9

Jenna stared at the screen until the data in front of her eyes began to scramble. There was something she was missing, and every minute she wasted was eating at her. She was close to picking up one of her monitors and hurling it across the room, even if going down to the gym and beating on one of the BOBs would be more effective.

It had been three days, and she felt as if she was going in circles every time she sat down at the computer. There were still three dead robots. They hadn't gotten word of any more, but there would be. It was only a matter of time, and it was her fault for not being able to figure it out.

The whole damn thing was her fault.

If she'd been stronger, if she'd been able to escape or resist making those protocols, these people wouldn't be dead. Maybe she wouldn't be unable to go outside either. Maybe she'd be a normal damned person and—

She forced herself to stop the thoughts running around in her head and stood, stretching. It was a rabbit hole she'd gone down plenty of times before, and she knew firsthand it didn't lead anywhere productive.

Heading to the kitchen, she turned on the coffeemaker. It was later than she normally had coffee, but sleep hadn't been her friend the last few days. Not that it ever was much of one.

It wasn't just the case causing her insomnia; it was the subconscious knowledge that someone else was in the house with her.

That was the thing, though. She didn't mind that Mark was around. For three days, they'd both been inside the confines of her home, and…it hadn't driven her crazy at all. She'd been pleasantly surprised by how comfortable it was.

When she'd offered him the spare bedroom, she'd been fully prepared to feel stifled and crowded. It had been a long time since she'd been around anyone for more than an hour or two at a time.

But it hadn't been that way at all.

Jenna actually liked having him around and found his presence comforting rather than annoying.

More than comforting.

But that wasn't something she could examine too closely. Not right now. Not ever. He already knew too much about her and what her life was really like.

She couldn't afford to let him know any more of the truth.

She got a mug out of the cupboard and grabbed the creamer from the fridge. She was barely able to handle her regression as it was. The idea of Mark knowing? Of seeing how far she'd fallen, even beyond what he'd already observed? She wasn't ready for it. Not that she ever would be.

And yet, having him here felt…*good*.

"Is that decaf?"

She jumped a little, gripping the creamer too tightly. At well over six feet and probably nearly two hundred pounds, the man could be absolutely silent when he wanted to be. He was lucky she hadn't put him on the floor.

Or the hospital.

She flinched. "Don't sneak up on me." That could be very dangerous for him.

"Sorry." Those green eyes pinned her, seeing way too much. "I thought you heard me."

"I didn't."

He nodded. "Understood. I'll be sure to let you know where I am from now on."

He didn't mock her for her overreaction or attempt to throw blame back on her. Neither did he brush off her response.

"You must think I'm a freak." She spun back around and poured creamer into her mug.

"I've served and worked with plenty of people who have their reasons for not wanting someone to come up on them unawares. I was careful not to make the mistake twice with them, and I'll be sure not to do it to you again either."

That was all she could really ask for, wasn't it? "Believe me, it's for your own safety."

"Roger that."

He didn't press. She was thankful.

"And no, the coffee isn't decaf. I felt like my brain was dragging fifty pounds of rocks behind it. Want some?"

"No, thanks. How's the work going?"

"It's not." She sighed, leaning back against the counter and taking a sip of the brew. "And it's driving me crazy. There's still nothing, and the fact that I can't pull together anything of substance—" She shook her head. "I should be able to. It's my work, for God's sake. Why can't I figure out why they're using it? The whole thing is my fault, and right now I can't do anything to stop it."

Mark leaned on the kitchen island and pinned her with a

sharp gaze. "Beat yourself up all you want, Jenna, but you can't be held responsible for what you were forced to do under duress."

She wasn't sure that was true. Things had happened, but she wasn't tortured. Not in the traditional sense, anyway. It wasn't lost on her that she was smart—a genius by most of the world's standards—and yet she still hadn't been able to figure out a way to fix the formula she'd developed or keep it from getting into the wrong hands.

And now, people were dead.

Her fingers gripped the mug way too tightly. She could feel tension spreading through her body. Adding coffee to her already spiraling system probably wasn't a good idea.

She looked up to find Mark staring at her hands.

"How about instead of drinking that, you and I go into the gym and spar?"

She hadn't sparred with anyone in over a year. She'd spent the first six months after her captivity learning everything she could about self-defense—sometimes spending six or eight hours a day in the gym where she lived in Denver.

Nothing had been more important to her than to feel safe.

Then, in one of the times she'd forced herself to go out of the house, some poor guy had made the mistake of coming up behind her and grabbing her shoulder as she was leaving the bar.

Her instincts—the good and the bad—had taken over. She'd broken his cheekbone, given him a concussion, and laid him out on the floor in seconds flat. He'd had to be taken to the hospital.

It had been Ian DeRose's high-end lawyers that had talked the guy out of pressing charges, explaining what Jenna had been through. Later, she'd found out Ian had also paid off all the guy's college loans.

How many times had she been over that scenario with her therapists?

The guy shouldn't have grabbed her like that.

She'd already been highly stressed because she was about to go back outside.

It was in the relatively early days after her release, and she didn't have as much control or focus as she did now. Her instincts had been to protect herself, an understandable impulse.

But Jenna knew the truth: her response had been nuclear.

And everyone staring at her that night like she was a monster—standing over a bleeding man she'd hurt for no reason—had confirmed it.

Yet another reason why she didn't leave the house much. She couldn't trust herself.

In the months since, she hadn't stopped her martial arts training. She'd needed it to remain sane. It was the only outlet her body had to get rid of the stress that sometimes felt like it was choking her.

If anything, she'd only gotten better. More deadly.

"Maybe sparring isn't a good idea." She put her coffee cup down. Caffeine probably wasn't a good idea either.

His eyes narrowed. "You afraid you'll lose?"

"The opposite, actually."

"I'm former Special Forces. I've gotten my ass handed to me by people a lot bigger and stronger than you. I know how to handle myself, and I think we both could use the physical activity."

He was right. He was more than capable of handling himself. She'd watched him on the Zodiac mission feeds more than once. He was every bit as good as her. Better.

"I can handle you, librarian." He crossed his arms over his muscular chest. "Let's do this."

"All right, Outlaw. I'll meet you there in five minutes. Let me change."

He nodded and headed toward his own room. She needed to prove to herself she could do this. Mark didn't need to know about the nuclear response incident. She didn't want him holding back or going easy on her because he was afraid of setting her off. That would defeat the purpose.

She slipped into her room and shut the door behind her. Her room was the one place she allowed her true tastes to rule. It had security to the gills, but it also featured softer colors and fabrics. An overstuffed armchair and an incredibly comfortable bed. The room was her sanctuary, and she'd gone to great lengths to make sure it was a sanctuary in every sense of the word.

Quickly, she changed into clothes to spar and put her hair up out of the way. Anxiety was still bubbling in her stomach, but she could do this. She needed to do this. Fighting didn't have to mean hurting anyone. She'd practiced enough on the BOBs, and she was confident she could defend herself. As long as nothing caused her to panic, she'd be fine.

Mark was already in the gym by the time she came down, moving around the equipment like he had been that first day. He was wearing gym shorts and a fitted blue T-shirt.

Confidence fairly dripped from him as he pulled the mats together and got the sparring dummies out of the way. Then he reached down and grabbed the backs of his calves, folding himself nearly in half. He then released his hold and moved into another stretch, then another as Jenna watched from the shadow of the doorway.

The slow, concise movements demonstrated strength, grace, and flexibility.

He'd been right. He could definitely handle her.

Not to mention there were other *physical activities* they could partake in to burn off some of this stress.

"We going to do this, or you just going to watch?"

He wasn't facing her, so she didn't know how he knew she was there, but he obviously did. She stepped more fully into the gym.

Sparring. Nothing else. Mark had no idea she thought about him like that. There had been a few moments when she thought she'd caught him looking at her over the past few days, but it had to be her imagination.

No one wanted to get involved with someone who couldn't even make it outside. That was ridiculous.

She grabbed her gloves and put them on. He put some on too.

"How hard do you want me to go?" Mark asked.

Jenna smiled at that. Nerves aside, this was going to be fun. "As hard as you like."

"Are you sure?" Mark stared at her.

"Very. I mean, I'd prefer not to die, but I can handle everything clsc."

He chuckled. "Not dying. Got it."

They faced each other then, both of them settled into low, ready stances that allowed them freedom of movement. Jenna immediately saw Mark's comfort in the gym wasn't merely for show. He was settled in his body, fully present, and all that sharp attention was focused on her.

He moved. Fast. He was so fast, coming at her with a quick strike she dodged purely on instinct. It was a test of her reflexes. Another quick movement put him closer to her, and she countered it. Another test. Despite asking her limitations, he was still testing them.

So Jenna made a move of her own. Three quick strikes to the torso that Mark blocked, backing on to the defensive, and she didn't stop, bringing her elbow to his face and stopping before she knocked him out.

Mark's face warmed into a smile. "Not bad, librarian."

"Told you." She grinned, backing away and giving him a chance to reset. "Now, are you going to stop toying with me and actually fight?"

"Yes, ma'am."

Jenna rolled her eyes. "The last thing I am is a ma'am."

He took advantage of the distraction, launching himself at her with speed she was envious of. But she was light on her feet, dancing backward and blocking two jabs at her face. She returned fire, landing one on his ribs before spinning away and maintaining distance.

Mark was fully grinning now. "Let's dance, Franklin."

And they did. Jenna knew Mark wasn't going full-out Special Forces on her, but he wasn't taking it so easy she felt insulted. She was making him work for every hit he landed and was landing enough of her own to feel like they were evenly matched. A few more months and he wouldn't have to hold back at all, if she kept up her work on the BOBs.

The thought made her confident. She stepped inside Mark's guard, throwing a punch that should have gone directly to the jaw; only he wasn't there anymore. He was on the floor.

At first, she thought it was a deliberate drop to escape the hit. But he didn't get up.

Dread crashed down on Jenna like one of the anvils in Saturday morning cartoons. Her mind flew back to that bar and the man she'd put on the floor, covered in blood.

What had she done? How had she managed to hurt someone this badly again? Her breath went short, and the world started to spin.

She was still a monster.

Fucking hell.

If peripheral neuropathy ever showed up in a human form, Mark was going to high-five it. In the face. With a chair.

It was so goddamned frustrating. Although right then, on the floor, his ego was bruised more than anything.

He'd felt the barest twinge of the motor nerve disorder when he started sparring with Jenna, but he'd ignored it. A lot of times, it never turned into anything more than the twinges. But sometimes, like right now, it reared its ugly head in the worst way. The muscle in his leg had collapsed, cramping and twitching and taking him to the floor before he knew it was coming.

It was everything he feared: one of his limbs stopping its correct function in the middle of a fight. What if it happened while he was on active status? While he was protecting someone? It could cost a life.

As much as he didn't want to complete the conversation he'd started with Ian about his physical limitations, Mark knew there wasn't much time left before his body made the choice for him. The knowledge burned like coals in his chest.

He looked up, expecting to find Jenna standing over him doing nothing short of a victory dance. And then he was going to have to explain to her what had just happened. He wasn't looking forward to that.

But instead, he found her pale, her eyes unfocused and distant like they'd been at the Eagle's Nest.

"No," she whispered. "Oh no."

"Hey, little librarian." He reached up and took her hand. "I'm fine. This wasn't because of you."

She shook her head back and forth slowly. "I was hitting you. I'm so sorry, Mark. I didn't mean to hurt you." Her words were shaky, broken. "Sometimes I just go into this zone and I don't know what I'm doing and—"

She was really upset. He wasn't sure exactly what was happening, but she was sinking into panic, and he wasn't going to let that happen.

He put his other hand around her hips and pulled her down to the floor with him, shielding her from the impact before he rolled over her body. Pressure was sometimes the best way to short-circuit a panic attack, and the only thing he had to use at the moment was his body.

"Hey."

She blinked up at him, awareness coming back to those brown eyes. "I hurt you. I didn't mean to. I—"

"Nope." Although, he wished that were the case. "Despite your impressive skills, you didn't do this. Sometimes I have... Sometimes I'll just have a thing where one of my muscles misfires. I've been dealing with it for a while, and I never know when it's going to happen. This wasn't your fault."

Some of the tension fell from her face. The knowledge she wasn't at fault was sinking in. "Really?"

"Really," he promised with a small laugh. "I was very much enjoying the fighting. My leg just had a problem. It was my own body that took me down. Not you."

"Okay." Jenna was biting her bottom lip, and the tiny motion made him even more aware of the position they were in. How soft and feminine she felt under him.

When she glanced at his lips and back up at him, he was done for.

Three full days being in this house with her, watching her be sassy, comfortable, and an absolute badass? Nearly every second had been a challenge not to kiss her.

Now, it would be damned impossible.

He moved closer, giving her every opportunity to pull

away, but she didn't. Those honeyed eyes dropped to his lips again, and that was it.

He kissed her.

Finally.

It felt like he was lit up within, along with everything else. Jenna's lips were perfect, and kissing her felt like the missing piece of a puzzle.

She kissed him back.

God, this was everything he'd imagined. Jenna wasn't shy or afraid; she was fire.

Her lips were soft and wet and open. Greedy. He loved it. He was greedy himself.

He slipped a hand behind her neck, pulling her closer. He wanted nothing more than to taste all of her, but he knew they had to take this slowly. For both their sakes. He made himself pull back and look at her.

Her eyes danced, and she had a smile on her lips. "I guess if you can kiss like that, I really didn't hurt you."

"You didn't. This is okay?"

She nodded. "Yeah. It's okay. More than okay. I just… need to take it slowly."

"Of course." Mark leaned in and stole another small kiss. "Just one more for the road."

He let her up, and she stood, brushing invisible dirt off her sparring clothes. "I guess I'm going to go to bed. You were right, this was better than drinking coffee if I want to get some rest." She cleared her throat and disappeared.

Mark was glad she couldn't see how wide his smile was as she walked away. There was something between them, and he was going to do his best to explore it. He would take all the time they both needed, but he wasn't going to shy away from whatever they were building.

But first, he needed a cold shower.

Chapter 10

Jenna blinked open her eyes. They currently felt like they had two-ton weights attached to them. Glancing over at the clock on the nightstand, she noted it was six in the morning.

She groaned. Why was she awake right now? She'd only gone to bed two hours ago, and even for her wonky sleep schedule, two hours was a bit slim.

Finally, the sound that woke her penetrated the haze around her brain. Her phone was ringing. Somewhere at the end of the bed, tangled in the blankets where she'd tossed it before collapsing, still in her clothes.

The number was blocked, but then again, most of her clients had blocked numbers for various reasons. "Hello?"

"I'm surprised you're awake."

Jenna recognized the voice and clenched her jaw. She was tempted to hang up but knew she couldn't. "Callum, it's six in the morning. It better be damned important. And why are you calling rather than sending a message."

He cut right to the chase. "This shit phone I have allows me to fly under Joaquin's security radar, but it has no internet connection. It can only make calls. We have a situation. There's another robot, but this one is alive."

"Alive?" All sleep fled. Her heart pounded in her ears.

A robot that was *alive*. Her brain ran over all the possibilities. Perhaps whoever programmed the robot forgot to put the tail in. Or if the tail had been edited into the robot's genes, maybe he or she had gotten lucky—had a genetic structure Joaquin's scientists hadn't calculated correctly.

If it had been Joaquin's people's mistake, he would rectify it quickly and kill the robot.

"Yes, alive. Male, twenty-three years old. Albuquerque. Ian already has his plane en route. It will meet you at the regional airport and take you to New Mexico."

She pressed her lips together. If Ian's plane was already on the way, it meant he knew and approved. His private plane was the only way she could get to Albuquerque in time to be useful. She wouldn't be able to get a commercial flight now, even if she was able to put herself through the trip—which she wasn't. She'd be a basket case by the time she arrived.

"Okay. We'll be there."

Callum disconnected without another word. She wasn't sure where he'd been calling from or if he was still undercover.

She took a deep breath and stood up from her bed. She had to move, couldn't afford to give her mind too much time to think or the fear would begin to suffocate her. Yes, she'd traveled on Ian's plane before and had been okay. But she couldn't forget that she hadn't even made it one minute outside a few days ago.

There was so much she couldn't control once she left the safety of this house. But still, *not going* wasn't an option. Not if she could save this person's life—separate the robot from the human.

She pushed out of her bedroom and padded across the house to Mark's room and knocked. The door opened a few seconds later, and Jenna was rendered completely speechless. Mark was there, staring down at the phone in his hand. He looked sleepy and tousled, with no shirt, and sweatpants that looked like they were clinging to his hips by the whisper of a prayer.

He looked up at her, eyes clear. "I just got a message from Ian that he's sending a plane. Are you all right?"

Jenna managed to tear her eyes from the body on display in front of her. She'd felt enough of it when he'd kissed her, but seeing all his bare skin was an entirely different experience, and she wished they didn't need to leave immediately. She'd be tempted to push him inside and find out if those muscles felt as delicious as they looked.

She shook her head, forcing away the thoughts. "Yes, Callum called. There's another robot in Albuquerque. Alive. They need me—" Her breath hiccupped, and she twisted her fingers to get the words out through the building anxiety. "They need me to get there to see if we can save him before his body starts shutting down. Thus, Ian's plane."

He glanced down at his phone. "Plane should be here in less than an hour."

"Guess we're going on a trip." She tried to force a smile.

"Are you going to be okay?"

"Do I have a choice?"

Mark sighed and cupped her cheek. "I guess not, but I'm going to do everything I can to get you through this. You're not alone. Not anymore."

She couldn't stop herself from leaning her cheek into his hand. "Thank you."

He stepped forward, pulling her to him and enveloping her in all his warmth. "You can do this. Right now, let's focus on getting everything we need together. One step at a time. Focus only on the step immediately in front of you."

She latched on to his words as he pulled away, kissing her forehead. She made herself move as they both dressed, and she set coffee on to brew. She packed up her two best computers for this type of job while Mark made them a small breakfast.

Each bite was torture, tasting like sawdust in her mouth, but she forced herself to. Her blood sugar bottoming out wouldn't do anything but make everything harder.

"Ready?" He grabbed both their bags.

She shook her head. "Not really. But let's go."

She didn't open the garage door to the outside until both car doors were shut. Mark had already been inside her SUV, but she noted the way he looked at it now, with a touch of awe.

"This thing really is impressive," he said.

"Thanks."

"I'm guessing the tech isn't the only bells and whistles?"

She allowed herself a smile, even through her tension. "That would be an understatement, but yes. A lot of custom security upgrades."

"Ditch the Fortune 500s," he said with a chuckle. "You could consult with the military and private security on vehicles like this."

"I've thought about it and have been approached more than once. But consulting on something like that would mean the specs are out there. You and I both know data like that isn't always safe. And if the specs are out there—"

"It could put you at risk," he finished. "I get it. Maybe once this danger has passed, you and I could work on something different. Something that's separate from your own security. Trust me, a lot of people would pay for these kinds of plans, and it would make the lives of people like me a lot easier."

People like him. Bodyguards for high-value targets.

Jenna swallowed. Here Mark was, guarding her even though he hadn't been ordered to. All her security was for her own peace of mind. She knew it was overkill in order to make her own mind feel safe.

Did Mark consider her to be a high-value target?

"In case I haven't said it, which I'm pretty sure I haven't...thank you for being here. For helping me. For putting up with me being a nutcase. I don't even know if you're getting paid—"

He reached over and grabbed her hand as she pulled out of the driveway and turned toward the airport. "Hey, you're not the only one who has a pretty nice nest egg. I could comfortably retire any time I wanted to. So let's not worry about getting paid. Let's worry about stopping Joaquin."

Jenna nodded but didn't say anything. She needed to focus on the road and keeping her panic at bay. She was already familiar with the regional airport they were driving to and knew she'd be able to pull her car all the way into the hangar then board the plane. The hangar was still an open structure, but it was a lot better than being fully outside and walking from a parking lot.

True to Ian's word, the plane was there and ready to go. She started to pull the SUV over to the side of the hangar where it could remain out of the way until they returned, and Mark held out a hand. "Let me." She looked over at him, and he smiled. "Just like the Eagle's Nest. Pull up close and go on board. I'll move the car out of the way and grab the bags."

She tightened her hands on the steering wheel, her relief at not having to fully face her fear warring with her need not

JANIE CROUCH

to rely on anyone. Relief won out. She killed the engine. "Thank you."

He said nothing as she pushed out of the SUV and quickly walked around the hood and up on to the plane. A woman met her inside. "Miss Franklin."

"Hi."

She nodded. "My name is Lyra. If you or Mr. Outlawson need anything, just let me know."

"I will, thank you."

Claiming a seat, she watched as Mark passed off their luggage to go in the belly and climbed the stairs. "We're good to go," he said to the pilot up front before coming back to join her.

Jenna saw him glance at the seats around her and choose the one across from her after a too-long look at the one beside her. He didn't want to crowd her, and she appreciated the impulse, but after this morning, she wanted to be closer to him. After takeoff, she would fix it.

One of the many benefits of flying in a private plane was the zero waiting. Within minutes of the cabin door being closed, the plane was making its way back to the runway and they were taking off. Jenna pulled the window shade. No doubt the sunrise over the Wyoming landscape was gorgeous, but she didn't want to take a chance on anything setting off a panic attack.

As soon as they were safely in the air, she unbuckled herself and squashed the nerves in her stomach. "Can I sit with you?"

Mark looked up from his phone and gave her a nod. "Always. You never need to ask."

She sat on the seat sideways, curling up so she could look at him. He was never going to be traditionally handsome—his face was too hard, too much of a warrior for that. Strong chin, carved jaw—both covered by a carefully trimmed

86

beard. His beard matched the thick brown hair her fingers itched to run through.

He made her feel safe.

The very fact that she was sitting there thinking about running her fingers through his hair rather than doing some breathing exercise to keep herself together was testament to that. Every other time she'd been on this plane, panic had been scratching at her the whole time.

Slowly, Mark reached out and took her hand. He rubbed his thumb over the backs of her fingers. "Can I ask you something?"

"Yes." She was surprised at how willing she was to give that answer.

He hesitated, and she sensed he was searching for the right words. "I know things are difficult for you with your agoraphobia, and I want to help you however I can. Can you tell me specific triggers? I'll do my best to keep you away from those things."

Jenna's breath stilled in her chest. Talking about it was terrifying, but for once, she actually wanted to. Mark had already seen her at her worst. If he wanted to help her, she should let him.

"I don't like to be outside," she said.

Mark laughed softly. Not *at* her, but simply a reaction. "I got that part."

She looked down at his hand cradling hers. "I'm fine in buildings and vehicles, clearly. Even windows don't bother me. But being outside or anywhere close to it…it sends me into a state of panic. Immediately and usually without recourse."

Lyra the flight attendant was headed toward them, but Mark waved her off. Again, his thumb smoothed over Jenna's skin, a careful, comforting gesture. "Can you give me specifics about why? I know about your captivity, but this feels like more than that."

She pulled her hand away and rolled up the leg of her pants before she took his again, guiding it to the skin of her ankle and the mottled scar there. "You feel that?"

He looked straight at her. "What is that?"

"It's…" She swallowed, shuddering, taking a moment to try to get herself under control.

"You know what?" he said. "Never mind. You've got enough on your plate without—"

"No," she cut him off. "You should know. Plus, my therapists all say it's good for me to talk about it if I can."

"Okay." His jaw was tight. He was preparing himself.

"When I was in captivity, whenever I didn't give Adil Garrison the results he wanted fast enough, he…"

She had to take a breath, chills running over her skin as she remembered the cold and the dark. The sounds. Garrison and his men had dragged her from the lab, through the wilderness, with only the headlights of the car to provide any light.

"Garrison would have his men take me to the middle of nowhere in the wilderness and tie me to a tree overnight. It was a joke to him. They used to make bets on whether I would be alive when they came back for me."

Mark's curse was low and foul. "Jenna—"

"I couldn't move. Couldn't get away. That scar on my ankle is from trying to get out of my restraints one night when I could hear wolves. I thought I was going to die."

Mark's face went slack with shock. "Jesus."

"Scratching myself bloody probably put me in more danger than if I'd just stayed still."

"How many times?" His jaw was tight. "How many times did Garrison do that to you?"

"I don't know. Over the course of the eighteen months,

maybe a dozen? The last time, it rained, and the temperature dropped so suddenly that I almost died from exposure and was useless to them for a couple of weeks. They stopped after that."

But by then, the damage had been done.

"I can only remember pieces of those nights. I remember screaming one night until my voice was gone. I remember one night when ants got on me and I couldn't get them off. And one night seeing a snake and thinking I would die. And those wolves. Or maybe those weren't all separate occurrences. I honestly don't know."

All she really knew was that the outdoors held all the things she was afraid of.

"Every time I step outside, I shut down and I'm right back there." She closed her eyes. "You were right. I'm not an introvert, I just let people think that. It's easier than explaining what a basket case I am."

Mark turned to her, hands coming up around her face. "Basket case?" He took a shaky breath, and she felt the tremor in his hands—the anger on her behalf. "Jenna, most people wouldn't be doing half as well as you are. The very fact that you can function at all is a miracle."

She shrugged. "It doesn't feel like much of a miracle."

"God, you're so fucking brave. I'm not sure I would be able to get out of bed in the morning."

"I don't feel like I'm doing well," she said, tears flooding her eyes and making him blurry. "I'm regressing. I was doing better, but then ever since that incident with Theodore Wilson, I can't even be outside for a full minute without throwing up. You saw me that day, balled up on the floor."

She tried to look away from him, but he tilted her face so she had nowhere else to look. "Theodore Wilson is an asshole of the biggest proportions, and if I had him here right now, I'd beat the shit out of him. He barged into your personal space and threatened to drag you out. Your reaction was understandable."

"I can't really even remember what happened afterward."

He kissed her forehead. "We got you calmed down, and I put you to bed. I stayed with you to make sure you were okay."

She couldn't look away from his intense green eyes. "I never said thank you for that either. I know you were in the middle of a big mission and probably didn't have time to waste with me being a basket case."

She couldn't look away from his intense green eyes. "You are never a waste of time for me. And as for a basket case, even without knowing what you just told me, I've never thought less of you. Not for one second."

She closed her eyes, and a tear spilled over. Mark gently brushed it away.

"I'm not going to push, but you have friends—people who are family in every way but blood—who would think nothing less of you either if you told them the details of your captivity."

"I know. But I'm not ready. Everyone was so happy to find out I hadn't been sexually traumatized. I don't want to let them know what I went through feels just as bad as I imagine that would have."

"That's because it was such a violation. You have the right to feel that way."

She'd never thought of it that way, but it made sense. "Thank you."

"I'd very much like to kiss you right now. I know we need to take it slow, and maybe this isn't the right—"

Jenna was the one to close the distance, desperate to be closer to him. When he'd kissed her in the gym, she'd been coming down out of her panic from thinking she'd hurt him, and still, it was incredible.

Now, she wasn't panicking, and this kiss…

It was safety and heat all at once. He tasted like the coffee they'd drunk that morning, and the way he moved had her wishing they were back at her house where they could do more than kiss.

He pulled her closer, like a man who knew exactly what he wanted.

And what he wanted was Jenna.

She felt small next to him but not vulnerable. All she wanted was to move closer. Except for a few brief hugs from her friends a few days ago, Mark was the only one who had touched her in months.

He was the one she thought about when she allowed herself to dream of having some kind of normal life. He was the one she thought about when she was afraid and needed to focus on regaining her calm.

Her fingers gripped his shirt, pulling him closer. She wasn't even sure if she was in control of her body doing it, and she didn't care. As long as he didn't stop making her feel like this.

He moved up the seat divider, and then his strong arm came around her, moving them so they lay across the seats, his body over hers in a way that was probably wholly inappropriate for the plane. But Jenna didn't care. She couldn't remember feeling so completely and entirely safe outside of her house.

Mark ran his hands down her body, guiding her legs apart so he could lie between them. But he didn't seem to be going further than that. Moving his mouth to her neck, he left a trail of kisses there. "It's unfortunate there are other people on this plane," he murmured into her skin. "Though

I know if there weren't, we wouldn't be taking this as slow as we should."

"Maybe I don't need slow," she said. "Maybe I just need you to keep kissing me, and when we're somewhere that doesn't belong to our boss, we'll see where things go."

Mark's smile was brighter than the sun streaming in the windows. "I can do that, little librarian."

He slanted his mouth across hers, and she got lost in his kiss. Nothing else mattered.

Chapter 11

They stayed tangled together until the flight attendant told them—while unnecessarily averting her eyes—that the plane was descending and they needed to buckle up. Nothing about what they'd been doing had been particularly scandalous, but Mark had a sparkle of amusement in his eyes as he helped her to sit up and buckled her in next to him.

Outlaw, indeed.

Jenna felt much steadier than she had when she'd boarded the plane, but she knew whatever they faced ahead might shake that steadiness quickly. Her nerves were already jangling about getting off the plane and into whatever car Ian sent. She was only truly comfortable inside her own vehicle—she knew its specs and trusted them.

Mark tucked an arm behind her and gently pulled her against his side, letting her lean on him. "You know I'm here for you, right?"

She smiled at him. "Yes."

She did know, and she appreciated it more than he knew. She was nervous right now, but not fighting back terror. That was thanks to him.

"Saving these people is important," he said softly. "Of course it is. But I'm here to be whatever you need and to keep you safe. You don't have to pretend with me, so if you need something you don't feel comfortable telling anyone else, tell me."

Jenna didn't know if she deserved that kind of consideration, but the words settled over her like a warm blanket, regardless. "Thank you."

The plane landed so smoothly she barely knew they were on the ground, and then they taxied toward the small buildings of this airport. In front of them, the flight attendant appeared once more.

"My apologies. Mr. DeRose wanted me to tell you that he's sorry this airport doesn't have a hangar large enough for this plane, but he hopes the vehicle he sent makes up for it."

Jenna's stomach plummeted, but Mark was already speaking. "Bring us as close as you can, please."

The woman nodded and went to tell the pilot.

"I'll go grab the keys and bring the car right next to the stairs."

"It's okay," Jenna said shakily. "They'll all look at me strangely if you do that."

"And?"

She couldn't come up with an answer. The shame she always felt about not being able to do things like walk out a door like a normal person bubbled up inside her. But this was her life. She couldn't change her paranoia, even with Mark at her side. And she needed to function once she got to wherever they were going, not be in recovery from a panic attack.

She hung her head. "Okay."

The plane stopped a few minutes later, and Mark went to do exactly what he'd said. Jenna sat still, her hands between her knees, trying to breathe and not think about how it would look and also not think about the unbearable amounts of space outside here in the middle of the desert.

She glanced out the window and did a double take. A vehicle was driving toward the plane, but it wasn't a car or an SUV like she'd expected. It was a bus. It looked like one of the giant buses bands went on tour in. Absolutely massive, with dark windows—a tint she recognized from her own car —and tires that were incredibly familiar.

Had Ian tricked out a tour bus for her?

Mark was smiling as he came out of the door right by the stairs, grabbing their luggage and taking it on board before he came for her. He was still beaming. "Good thing I have a Class A driver's license. But you are going to love this thing."

"I'm sure I will," she muttered. "I just have to get there first."

"I have an idea." He sank onto one knee in front of her. "The bus is already at the bottom of the stairs. Will it help at all if I carry you? You can close your eyes, you'll only be outside for a few seconds, and you don't have to worry about anything else."

She knew what walking down even the few stairs of the plane was going to feel like. Knew about the dizziness that was going to assault her. The vomiting by the time she made it to the bottom of the steps.

The terror that was going to feel like it was ripping through her from the inside out.

Normally, having other people nearby as she tried to go outside made everything worse because she was trying to hide her reaction and live through it. But Mark already knew.

Having him carry her would be weird—and certainly would appear odd to the flight crew. But it would hopefully allow her to keep her breakfast and not lose hours to the panic.

She nodded. "Okay."

Without another word, he slipped an arm under her legs and behind her shoulders and lifted her like she was nothing. Jenna had felt his body plenty while they were tangled up on the seats, but feeling his strength in this way was different, and she didn't mind it. At all.

"I like this," he said quietly, echoing her thoughts. "Now, close your eyes."

She did. The sun hit her face first, and she turned instinctually, curving into Mark's hold. The desert air was dry and hot, and she felt the sun on her skin. Dizziness spun through her even though her feet weren't on the ground, and the gentle breeze made goose bumps rise on her arms.

There had been wind out there too. It had howled across the ground and made her freeze. The glowing eyes in the dark—

A sound cut off her thoughts, mechanical in nature. "Here we are," Mark said. "The door is already closed. You made it."

She waited, swallowing, catching her breath. *She'd made it.* Thanks to him.

Jenna opened one eye, about to thank him, but then gasped as she caught sight of the vehicle they were in. This was more than just a bus. Mark slowly set her down.

It was a command center on wheels. A six-monitor setup with a big desk sat along one wall, all idling on the Zodiac Tactical home screen. There was a stove and a refrigerator, and farther down, she saw a bed through a door all the way at the back and what looked like an incredibly comfortable couch. Further exploration showed her the couch was across from a massive television, which could be connected to the monitor setup.

"Ian left some info," Mark said as she walked around. "This thing has most of the same security specs your personal vehicle does. Bulletproof glass, slash-proof tires, coded locks, the works."

This was a place she could be away from home and feel entirely safe.

"Ian never does anything by half measures, does he?" she asked, awed.

Mark laughed. "No, he certainly doesn't. He also cares a lot about you. Don't forget that. You've got more friends than you know."

She nodded. This wasn't a thing you could wake up and order to be dropped off the same afternoon. Ian had prepared this for her well in advance. She owed him a big thank-you.

"Ready to hit the road? Callum's waiting. I'll drive if you want to go through the most recent intel he sent."

"Sure." She sat down at the giant workstation. The chair was on wheels, but it also had buttons that locked it to the floor for when the bus was moving, and a seat belt.

Mark strapped into the driver's seat, and she fired up the computers. While they drove, she located the file from Callum on the latest robot.

Brett Cochran, twenty-three. He didn't live in Albuquerque; he was from Los Angeles. According to the files they'd pulled on him, he was an aspiring actor. So why the hell was he in Albuquerque, attempting to rob an art gallery?

Jenna shook her head. It barely made sense. Sure, as much as she hated it, she understood the logic of the bad guys using her creation to do bad things. But so far, the crimes seemed petty. Not only were they not successful, they seemed random.

It seemed like very little payoff for a lot of work.

Callum had already run Brett Cochran. So far, there didn't seem to be any link between him and the other robots.

Jenna would dig into that more later, to make sure nothing had been missed.

For the rest of the drive, she worked on setting up her safety protocols for the workstation and fired off a thank-you email to Ian. By the time the bus was pulling into the hospital, she'd nearly forgotten she was going to have to go outside again.

"I'm going to pull up to the front entrance," Mark said from the driver's seat. "It'll only be a few feet to the front door, and someone will be there to meet you."

"Okay."

She was almost tempted to ask if he could carry her again, but there wasn't time for that. They were here, and the robot's life hung in the balance. This was her mess, and no matter how emotionally screwed up she was, she had to fix it.

She stood by Mark as he pulled up to the entrance of the hospital. He reached over and squeezed her hand. "You can do this. I'll be in in a couple of minutes."

Nodding, she didn't meet his eyes. She simply turned and punched in the code for the door, locking her eyes on the hospital doors in front of her.

The second her feet hit the ground, she felt the panic swarm her body. The bitter taste of adrenaline coated her tongue. There was too much space, too much space, too much space. Her heart slammed against her ribs as she sprinted to the doors and rushed inside, barely missing running into an elderly couple who was leaving.

They smiled at her gently, obviously convinced she was rushing in to see someone. Little did they know they'd nearly been the latest victims of her inability to control her emotions and panic.

She mumbled an apology and moved farther away from

the door. A woman caught her eye and rushed toward her. "Jenna Franklin?"

"That's me." She somehow managed not to sound like she about to keel over.

"My name is Lauren Marino. I work with Callum Webb. He wanted me to make sure you have everything you need."

Jenna nodded. "Sounds good. Lead the way, but Mark Outlawson is here with me. Can you make sure he knows how to find me?"

"Of course."

Lauren started walking, and Jenna followed. Now that she was inside and her heart was calming, everything was much better. Her mind was clearing, and she was thinking about what she was going to need.

"We have a lab set up for you and ready to go," Lauren said. "Hopefully it has everything you need to run your tests."

"Okay. I'll need new blood samples and vitals as soon as possible."

"We'll get them for you."

Lauren opened the door to the lab, and once again, Jenna had to take in a breath to settle herself. Yes, she had a PhD in bioengineering, but that wasn't much a part of her daily life any longer. Since her captivity, she'd moved her focus over to her other degree: computer science.

Jenna gritted her teeth and slipped on the lab coat hanging by the door. She categorically refused to lose this like she'd lost the ability to go outside. She was needed, and it didn't matter if the last time she'd worked in a lab wasn't of her own free will.

The county hospital was small, and the lab wasn't extensive or polished, but they'd done well to pull the equipment she needed on such short notice. It would have to do.

"If you're all right," Lauren said, "I'll grab your friend

and make sure all info and samples are routed directly to you."

"Thank you."

Jenna didn't look up as the woman exited. The previous samples were already logged, but the tests she needed hadn't been run. There wasn't a lot of time if she was going to save Brett Cochran's life.

Jenna started working, autopilot kicking in as she ran tests and began analyzing Brett's genes and responses to the genetic manipulation. She heard Mark enter, but he stayed out of the way, letting her work. The hours flew by with test after test as Jenna tried to combat the tail that had been left in the robot's system.

Not robot—Brett. Brett Cochran. Barely more than a kid.

He wasn't Joaquin's robot anymore; he was a person. But his system was shutting down.

A nurse brought in the latest blood work, and Jenna ran it through her system.

"Shit."

One glance at the clock told her it was early evening and she'd barely noticed the hours passing. A cup of coffee sat next to her, and she didn't remember how it got there.

"What's wrong?" Mark asked.

"Nothing we're doing is helping. Brett is getting worse."

"Is it the tail like you were mentioning before? That's what's killing him?"

Jenna pulled up the video image of Brett's room. "He's dying. And the tails don't kill the victims exactly. The tail is a splice that creates an addiction. Except a normal addiction is like a wave, and a tail is more like a tsunami. It makes the host completely dependent on the chemicals, and if they don't get them, they die. Deadly withdrawal."

"Fuck," he said quietly. "But you figured out the tail is there. That's good, right?"

She turned off the footage of Brett. "Yes, it's good that I figured out it's in there, but this isn't my work. Or rather, it's not only my work. The tail has been tweaked, and I have no idea what combination of chemicals his body needs to keep him alive."

Mark winced. "How long do we have?"

"Hours, at most. Like I said, he's getting worse." Dread and panic flowed into her system. This was her fault. She'd created this protocol, and if she couldn't crack it, that young man would die. "I'm going to try what I can. If I hit on what works, it will help immediately, but—"

Mark stepped forward into her space, reaching up to take her face in his hands. "Take a breath for me." She did. "You're going to try. And if you find it, it's amazing. If you don't, it is not your fault."

"You know that's not true."

His face hardened. "That's not something we'll argue about now. Tell me what you need."

"Nurses," she said. "I'm going to create samples based on the data I have, and they're going to need to administer the compounds and report back with Brett's reaction. I need people going back and forth so I don't have to leave the lab —it'll be hit or miss for a number of hours until he reacts and I get us going in the right direction."

Leaning in, he kissed her briefly. "You got it. Now put everything else out of your mind. What you can do is all you can do."

What she could do was all she could do.

Jenna connected Brett's heart rate to her computer, and she watched it get weaker as the hours bled into the night and the combinations she could think of to combat the tail dwindled.

Multiple nurses came in for instructions and to provide results. They were quick and efficient.

And useless. Because Jenna couldn't figure out the tail.

Maybe if someone took her out into the wilderness and tied her to a tree for a few hours, she'd work better—that had certainly been effective the first time.

"Here, I'll take the next one."

Something landed on her shoulder, and Jenna reacted, spinning and hitting the object with fast and brutal force. The gasp made her vision clear, and she saw the nurse in front of her, cradling her arm to her chest like she'd been bitten.

"Oh my God." Jenna choked on the words. "I'm so sorry. Did I hurt you? I'm so sorry. Are you okay?"

Terror laced the pit of Jenna's stomach as the nurse rubbed her arm, scooting away from her.

"I'll live. But cut down to decaf before you take someone out, okay?"

Jenna handed her the latest syringe and couldn't help but notice the sideways glance the nurse gave her as she left. Jenna deserved that, almost breaking the poor woman's arm for touching her on the shoulder.

Some things didn't change.

Mark passed the nurse on the way in, looking at Jenna with raised brows. He had a brown paper bag in his hand and another cup of coffee. "Everything okay?"

"Fine."

"You don't look fine. That nurse didn't look fine."

"She startled me, and I hurt her arm."

Mark was silent for a long moment, obviously running scenarios in his head.

"You need to eat," he finally said. "You've been working nonstop all day. Coffee can only take you so far."

Jenna swallowed. "I don't have time to eat." The last

couple of batches had produced a slight response. She was going to build from there, but it would take time. Probably another two hours before she had anything that would definitively start helping Brett.

She turned away from the food and Mark and went back to work, not mentioning what had happened with the nurse. She didn't have time to explain to him yet another way she was broken.

Her eyes flicked to Brett's heart rate monitor in the corner of her screen, and she watched it flicker, then plummet. "No."

Before she even realized, she was sprinting out of the lab and into the stairwell—the elevator would be too slow. Up three floors and down the hall to Brett's room. She heard Mark running behind her, but she didn't stop.

The chaos could be heard from down the hall—yelled commands and the shrill, insistent sound of a flatline.

No. No, no, no.

She skidded to a stop outside Brett's room, watching as a doctor and the nurses she'd been handing syringes to all day worked over Brett's body. Even the nurse with the hurt arm was helping, pushing the injury aside.

Mark stopped beside her. "I'm too late," Jenna said. "He won't make it. He's too weak, and I didn't figure out how to help him."

The doctors and nurses tried. They tried using manual methods alongside the defibrillator to get Brett's heart beating again.

But Jenna knew it wasn't going to happen. His heart had already been weak without the correct cocktail, and in the absence of the chemicals his body had been programmed to need in order to exist, he wouldn't make it.

She stood there, transfixed, watching until the doctor

finally pulled himself away and looked at the clock on the wall, calling the time of death.

Brett Cochran was dead. *All she could do* was what she had done.

And it hadn't been enough.

Chapter 12

Mark pulled the bus up to the door of the hospital and carried her on board, just like he had from the plane. He loved the feeling of her in his arms. What he didn't love was seeing Jenna both exhausted and trying to destroy herself from the inside out.

Sealing the door behind him, he set her gently on her feet. "You need some rest. I'm going to drive us to a spot we can park safely."

While she'd been working in the lab, he'd made sure they had a place to go. They couldn't just leave the bus parked at the hospital doors. There was an RV parking lot not far away, which would be fine. Plus, the bus Ian had provided was a fortress on wheels. Mark was more worried about getting a ticket than being in danger from anything outside the bus, except for maybe a nuclear blast.

Parking in the RV lot, he shut down the bus and went back into the main part of it, fully expecting Jenna to be passed out on the bed. She'd barely eaten all day, working at a frenzied pace that would have put most people on the floor.

He could see she was exhausted, but she wasn't asleep. She was sitting cross-legged on the bed, staring at the floor.

"Not tired?"

Her eyes lifted to his, and she shrugged. It was a nonanswer, because she couldn't lie about that. Her shoulders were drooping with fatigue, but she didn't look like she was remotely ready to sleep.

He slipped off his shoes and set them next to hers before he climbed onto the bed and sat next to her. "Want to talk about it?"

She sighed. "What is there to talk about? Another person is dead because of me."

"Hey—"

"No," she said, finally turning to fully look at him. "We can dance around this all we want, but this is my fault. I designed the conditioning program years ago. I engineered the way to hijack people's brains and let them be taken away from themselves. Not only that, but I'm the one who made it so they won't ever remember what happened to them, and that whoever takes control of them can addict their bodies to chemicals they'll need for life."

Her voice cracked.

His heart broke.

She'd already been through so much with her captivity— the things she'd told him about on the plane had him wanting to put his fist through a wall.

Or to carry her everywhere she needed to go for the rest of her life.

To have that trauma plus what she'd been forced to create while kidnapped come back to haunt her over and over… It seemed too much for anyone to bear.

"And I couldn't save Brett." She swiped at her eyes. "Not only could I not save him, I basically killed him. I hurt everybody."

Her eyes were wild as she bolted off the bed, pacing across the tiny space like a caged tiger.

Mark had plenty he wanted to say, logical arguments he wanted to make for all the reasons she wasn't at fault. But he'd spent enough time around men and women suffering from the emotional fallout of PTSD to know that logic didn't mean shit to her right now.

She needed someone to listen, so he stayed silent. He never took his eyes from her so she knew she had his full attention.

"Do you know why I panicked when you fell during our spar? Because a few months after my release, someone touched me when I wasn't expecting it, and I put him on the ground. I broke his cheekbone and gave him a concussion. All because he touched my shoulder and caught me off guard. I'm lucky he didn't press charges."

That explained a lot. Mark could point out that the guy probably hadn't pressed charges because anybody with an ounce of compassion would understand that her reaction had to do with her captivity. But again, he wasn't going to be able to logic Jenna out of this.

"Back in the hospital," she continued, "one of the nurses did the same thing while I wasn't paying attention, and I nearly broke her arm. How long is it going to be before it's not just the robot stuff that's killing people, but I kill someone because I'm distracted and my body acts first? It seems like no matter what I do, I hurt people."

"And you thought you'd hurt me while we were sparring."

She spun, hands on hips. "Yes. That would be par for the course, don't you think? This is why I shouldn't go outside! Not just because I'm a basket case, which I most definitely am, but because when I do, people get hurt!"

She ran out of steam all at once, breath heaving.

"Come here," he said, patting the bed beside him.

Jenna did, avoiding his eyes. He shifted them both so they were facing each other. That was all a lot, but it wasn't anything unexpected. "We can talk about all of this as much as you want, either now or at a later date," he said. "But there's one thing I need to say, and I need you to hear me when I say it."

The words made her look up at him, and if Mark could have had one wish granted in that moment, it would have been to remove the terror from her eyes.

"There is no shame in having trauma, Jenna."

Her whole body shuddered. "But—"

"No," he said gently, unable to resist the urge to reach out and touch her any longer. He wrapped an arm around her shoulders and pulled her toward him. She came to him willingly, leaning on him, and the relief of holding her made him breathe easier.

"Someone took you, and they hurt you. They forced you to do the unfathomable while threatening your life in ways that the average person couldn't even wrap their head around. You were tortured."

She shook her head. "I wasn't. Not really. I—"

"Maybe you weren't tortured in a traditional manner, but you were still tortured. What Garrison did to you out in those woods? Leaving you alone there? Psychological torture, with some physical torment thrown in."

"But I—"

He put a finger gently over her lips. "There is no world where you're not a victim too, and you have nothing to be ashamed of for existing with what has been done to you. You survived, and survival is always the most important thing. But you will also be dealing with the fallout from this trauma for the rest of your life."

She didn't say anything, but when she tucked her face

into his shoulder, he ran his fingers into her hair to keep her there.

"Did you do everything you could today?"

"I should have been able to figure out what Joaquin changed," she said into his neck. "It's my work. Why couldn't I see the missing piece?"

He smoothed a hand up and down her spine. "That's not what I asked."

She hesitated, but finally, she eased back a little so they were able to look into each other's eyes. "Yes, I did everything I could."

"And did you mean to hurt that man when you were first released? Or the nurse today?"

"No. But I still did. And I'm afraid I'll do something worse."

Mark held her for a moment, trying to find the correct words for what he wanted to say and ask. "Is that another reason why you stay away from people? Even those you care about?"

Slowly, she nodded. He held her tighter, and his chest ached for everything Jenna had against her right now. Fear on every side, and not just plain fear. Terror that twisted your brain until you were your own enemy in your mind.

"You're not superhuman," he finally said. "You have an absolutely incredible mind, and you kick ass with your fighting skills, but you're still human. Humans are allowed to be afraid. We're allowed to make mistakes. We're allowed to do the best we can without feeling like a failure."

"I did fail. Brett died." He heard tears in her voice.

"Play pretend with me for a moment. Let's say it wasn't you who created the genetic modification program, the chemical tails that are so deadly, and everything else—someone else did it. Let's say Joaquin got his hands on those other formulas and managed to tweak them to his own satisfaction and created his robots that way. Those people would still die, and Joaquin is the one who killed them."

Mark turned Jenna's face to the side and brushed away the tears on her cheeks. He couldn't bear her misery. "I'm not saying those people dying isn't a tragedy. It is. But I'm asking you to put the blame where it belongs: squarely at the feet of the monster subjecting people to this."

"But it wasn't some imaginary biochemical engineer who designed these methods. It was me."

"I know it was. But the truth is, if you'd died out in those woods one night, Adil Garrison would've found someone else to complete your work. We both know that's the case."

She nodded slightly.

"Joaquin is no fool. He had someone build on the methods you created and change them so you couldn't stop him. He wants you to feel helpless. Wants you to think there is nothing you can do."

"He may be right," she whispered.

"I'm betting he's wrong. The progress you made with Brett today will be applicable to the next robot, right?"

"Yes, it should be."

"Then as sad as Brett's death is, at least some good came out of it."

He saw the knowledge settle into her, and though he knew it wouldn't fix everything, he hoped she would be able to let herself breathe.

"What can I do?" he asked quietly. "What can I do to help you?"

Jenna took a shaky breath and looked at him. "I don't want to think," she said. "I want to get out of my own head. I want us to continue what we started on the plane today."

He stared at her, gauging her seriousness. Jenna was everything he wanted, but like hell was he going to do something she would regret later. "Are you sure?"

"Yes." Those honey-colored eyes were clear. Earnest.

Closing the distance between them, he kissed her, and it wasn't gentle. Internally, he thanked the tiny arrogant part of him that had hoped this might happen and thought to pack condoms. "Okay."

He pulled away long enough to retrieve one, and when he returned to the bed, Jenna was peeling out of her shirt and wiggling out of her pants. For one miraculous second, he was struck dumb, seeing more of her skin than he ever had and feeling the way she looked at him, with both weight and heat.

His mind was running wild with all the possibilities of what he wanted to do to her. With her. Anything and everything.

He wanted to take her against every surface in this bus, and more besides. Lay her out on those same gym mats where they sparred and worship her until she forgot all her fear and even her own name.

Pulling off his shirt, he tossed it aside and enjoyed the way her gaze trailed over his chest. She'd seen him shirtless before, but it was different now.

Reaching out, he grabbed her ankle and pulled her to the edge of the bed, putting everything he wanted within his grasp. Mark leaned down, brushing his mouth across her belly. "Tell me what you like."

A shivering gasp rushed out of her as he kissed across her chest. "I can't even remember."

"Liar," he said, smiling into her skin. "Don't be afraid, Jenna. If you want this and want me, trust me. Tell me how to drive you wild."

She sank her hands into his hair and pulled his mouth to her. "Tonight? I just don't want to think about anything. I don't want to answer questions, I just want to feel. Feel you. Feel us."

"I can do that." There was nothing he wanted more.

Running his lips over her skin once again, he touched her, easing his hands up along her ribs until he reached her bra and removed it. If she wanted to feel, he would make her feel. Take some time—not all the time he wanted, that would be all night—but time to explore her the way he'd been craving for so long.

When he knelt before her at the edge of the bed, he felt a little like a man come to worship, and he didn't mind it for a second. If anyone deserved to be worshipped, after everything she'd been through, it was Jenna.

He removed her underwear, parted her legs, and consumed her, listening to the sounds she made and the way she breathed, guiding her toward pleasure.

Long and slow, he devoured her, taking his time, enjoying the feeling of her fingers in his hair, dragging his mouth closer and wordlessly asking for more with moans and sighs. When her orgasm came, it wasn't explosive—she was too emotionally and physically exhausted. Instead, it was a sigh that had her body arching and shaking and finally relaxing. So when he stripped off the rest of his clothes and fit himself against her, the only thing Jenna was thinking about was him. He saw it in her eyes.

They both groaned as he pushed in, and it felt like more than just sex. It felt like the connection they'd both been needing and not been able to admit. Jenna's eyes were only for him, and he didn't look away.

Firm and steady, rolling his hips, he did all he could to hold on and make it last. They didn't need any words between them now. It was just them and the sensation of being the only two people in the world.

Mark kissed her, clinging to control by a thread as she shuddered underneath him, whispering his name into their kiss. Hearing it from her lips made him let go, pleasure raging through him like a storm.

They came to stillness together, breathing each other's breath and not daring to move, neither wanting to break the tiny spell that had been woven around them.

But eventually, they had to move. Mark finally saw the exhaustion taking root in Jenna. Gently pulling away, he cleaned himself up, and her, before lifting her higher onto the bed and wrapping them in blankets. Jenna didn't resist, turning into his chest, her breath slowing. He thought this might be the most relaxed he'd ever seen her.

"Thank you," she whispered.

He pressed a kiss to her forehead. "You don't ever have to thank me for this, Jenna."

He would happily do this for the rest of his life.

But Jenna was already asleep.

Chapter 13

It was the sound of a keyboard that woke Mark. Light was leaking into the bus around the corners of the blackout blinds in place in the bedroom, and Jenna was no longer next to him.

Mark sat up, able to see her through the open door. She was sitting at the giant workstation, a cup of coffee beside her, and wearing only his shirt. The sight of her bare legs peeking out from under his T-shirt was enough to make him want to pull her out of that chair and drag her back to bed.

But the second thing he noticed was her focus. In the few days he'd been living at her house, he noticed she didn't sleep much, but he'd also come to observe different versions of Jenna. And the woman rapidly typing on the keyboard, full of sharp, barely contained energy, was a very different version from the exhausted, devastated woman he'd held in his arms last night.

Something was up.

Finding his pants on the floor, he pulled them on before he walked out and leaned against the wall closer to her. "Good morning."

She didn't look up from the screen. "Morning."

No. That wasn't going to do at all. He bent down so he was right in front of her and kissed her. And not what he would normally consider a good morning kiss.

He took possession of her mouth and didn't stop until both of them were breathing hard. When he pulled back, those brown eyes of hers were soft and a little unfocused.

"Good morning," he said again.

He loved the gentle smile she gave him. "Good morning."

He straightened. "How are you feeling?"

"As good as I can after yesterday's fiasco, I suppose. I don't know if I can fully let go of what happened, but I feel a little better." She turned back to the screen. "When I woke up, I had a thought."

"How long have you been up? And what was the thought?"

"Not long. And I was thinking about motivation. So far, we have four people with no discernible connection. I cross-referenced Brett with the other three robots."

Mark walked over to pour a cup of coffee. "I assume he didn't provide any magical connection."

"No, nothing. No links to any of the others at all. Which didn't surprise me. So instead, I started to really look at the places the robots were robbing."

He took a sip. "A couple of jewelry stores, a pawn shop, and an art gallery."

"Right. The thing is, nothing was really taken from any of them. Whether it was because law enforcement got there first, or that was never the plan, it seems strange, right?"

Mark nodded. "Yeah. Using something like chemical subjectification in order to rob relatively low-value targets seems like overkill."

"Yeah, that was my thought too. Joaquin is too smart to

be spending so much time and money for so little payoff. He's creating these robots for more than smash and grabs all over the country."

"Agreed. Did you figure anything out?"

"Only that I was looking at things wrong in terms of the robots' connections," Jenna said.

She clicked a few things on her keyboard, and all four victims, including Brett Cochran, popped up on one of the monitors. "I was looking for traditional connections—someone they all knew or an organization they were all a part of. That was a dead end."

"But you found something else?"

"Yes. All four of them have some sort of computer expertise."

She stood and pointed to the first and third victims. "This gal was a computer science major in college, and this guy was a programmer. I spotted that early on but discounted it because the second victim and Brett didn't seem to have any computer-related ties. But I was wrong."

"How so?"

"Our second victim was a struggling actor in LA. He had all sorts of jobs, one of them as a computer repair technician in between auditions."

Mark sat up straighter. "What about Brett? Any connection to computers?"

"It didn't look like it. Dude didn't even have so much as a social media presence—almost unheard of for a twenty-three-year-old. He was studying British Literature in college, which is like the polar opposite of computers."

"So, no link?"

She clicked a few more keys. "I'm hoping you'll stand by your Outlaw nickname and not mind this too much since it's technically illegal, but I dug into Brett a little more. Ends up he had a sealed juvenile record. Little fifteen-year-old Brett made some bad choices. *Hacking*."

"Oh shit." All the victims *were* connected.

"Yep. I wouldn't have found it if I hadn't dug. Evidently, Brett had put his evil hacking ways behind him, or at least had convinced the law he had. But all four victims had pretty extensive computer knowledge."

"So, rather than breaking in to these places for their jewelry or cash, you think they did something to each business's computer system?"

She shrugged. "I have no idea what, but it makes more sense than Joaquin sending them in to grab whatever's in the cash register. Do you think we could get access to Brett's crime scene?"

"Yeah. I'm sure Callum and his Omega Sector team can circumvent any jurisdictional issues we might have. We can go right now."

Some of the color bled out of her face. "Great."

"You don't have to go. I can look and report back."

Jenna shook her head, pressing her lips together. "That won't work. If they were accessing the computers, I need to be there to see what was done. I'm just going to have to deal with a little bit of going outside."

"Jenna." He spun her fully to face him. "The last twenty-four hours have been very stressful for you. It's okay to sit this one out."

She shook her head. "All I can do is what I can do, right? I can do this. I promise I'm not trying to torture myself, but I owe it to these people to try to figure out why they died and try to stop it from happening to anyone else."

This woman. She was so much stronger than she gave herself credit for.

He tilted her face up and dropped a kiss on her lips. "I'll do whatever I can to make it easier for you."

"I know."

Less than a half hour later, they were pulling up outside the art gallery Brett Cochran had broken into. A bus this size looked entirely out of place against the curb here, but Mark didn't care. He was minimizing the distance for Jenna.

The cop on duty didn't even blink at them as Mark carried Jenna from the bus inside the gallery. Jenna hadn't questioned when he held his arms out—but even then, he felt her breath go short and saw her eyes squeeze tight against the sun's brightness and the open feeling of fresh air when they stepped outside.

"Okay, we're in," he said when the door shut behind them.

The building was blocked off with crime scene tape, but it didn't look like a typical crime scene. Sure, stuff was broken. Glass had been smashed and things toppled over. But none of the art had been touched. It didn't even look as if there had been an attempt to remove any of what was on display.

Jenna slid down from his arms and began to walk toward the back.

"What are we looking for?"

"The office," she said.

He followed her back to find that room had been trashed like the gallery, but the computer hadn't been harmed. Jenna stepped over the scattered papers and overturned filing cabinet, dragging a chair in front of the computer.

"I'm going to look around some more while you do your thing."

"Okay." She didn't look up from the screen.

He walked back into the gallery, looking at the art in case

the content was at all relevant. It was beautiful, but somehow he didn't think the abstract paintings of southwest mesas were Joaquin's ultimate goal.

What was his ultimate goal? The inside of this building looked more like teenagers had gone on a drunken rampage than an actual attempt at theft. Mark slowly walked through the gallery but didn't see anything that provided insight as to what the true plan had been. He made his way back into the office.

"Any luck?"

Jenna blew out a breath, a crease growing between her eyebrows. "There's nothing on this thing worth stealing. And there's evidence of a breach, but why? The computer was accessed during the break-in, but other than client data and the gallery's financials, I don't see anything that would give Joaquin motivation to send a robot in here."

Mark looked around, evaluating the office from both a safety and an architectural perspective. "Keep looking," he said. "Be absolutely sure."

She kept staring at the monitor. "Yeah."

Something about this room was bugging him, and he wasn't sure what it was.

He stepped back out of the office and looked down the hall to the rear of the building. It went maybe twenty more feet, with what looked like a utility closet behind the office. He walked over and opened the door. Nothing unusual. Shelves with cleaning supplies, a bucket and a mop, what appeared to be a few alternate displays for things like sculptures and three-dimensional art pieces.

But it didn't run the length of the office. The office was at least twelve feet across, and the closet was eight deep at most. He stepped inside and pressed a hand to the back wall.

It was warm. The wall that shared the office was cool.

It was possible that the space behind the closet was used

by the business next door, but design-wise, it didn't make sense.

Going back to the office, Mark went straight to the bookshelf covering the extra "empty space." It wasn't like the detective movies where there were scratch marks on the floor showing that the shelf was movable. No, he was pretty sure no one had moved this bookshelf in years and hadn't wanted to.

Bracing himself against the wall, he shoved the shelf, moving it about a foot. Yeah. There it was. A doorframe.

"What are you doing?" Jenna asked.

"Following a hunch."

He shoved the shelf again, and Jenna jumped up to help him. Together, they moved the shelf across the back wall, and Mark thanked the universe that his body was cooperating today. He felt no tingles or weakness, and he wanted it to stay that way.

Once they got the bookshelf out of the way, they could clearly see the door. It was locked with a keypad.

"Well, damn, Outlaw," Jenna said, tracing her hand softly over the keypad. "Looks like you just found the jackpot."

"How so?"

"That keypad makes the ones on my house, car, and the bus look like children's toys. And that door? It would take a bazooka to get through it. I'd be willing to bet the walls are made of something similar. This is the kind of tech I'd expect to see on…" She froze and turned back to the computer. "Hold on."

As she sat back down, her fingers flew across the keyboard faster than he could see, opening up coding windows and flipping through screens he could barely process.

"Wow, I can't believe this," she whispered. "You should always trust your hunches, Mark."

He laughed. "What is it?"

"I think you may have just cracked the case, but I want to be sure before I even say it out loud. I need to get back to my computer."

They did, with Mark carrying her inside the bus once again. But Jenna didn't have quite the same reaction this time. She was focused, fully intent on what she was doing. As soon as they got back in, she jumped in front of her computer.

He let her work, ignoring the mutters she made to herself. He'd worked with her at Zodiac enough to know that staying out of her way was the best thing he could do. She would tell him as soon as she had something.

"We were right," she finally said. "Smash and grab wasn't Joaquin's plan."

Mark dragged a chair over so he could sit next to her. "What did you find?"

"Behind that door in the office is one of the remote backup servers for the IRS."

His eyebrows rose into his hairline. "What?"

"It's not entirely uncommon, and it's not just the IRS. Government agencies have partial server backups in civilian buildings everywhere for, well...backup reasons. They don't announce the servers' locations because that would defeat the purpose. What better place to hide them than in nonofficial buildings?"

"And the owners know?"

Jenna gave a one-shouldered shrug. "I doubt it. It's like when you have some sort of utility box on your house's property—the owner doesn't know what it is or what it does, just knows he's not supposed to mess with it. The owners of the art studio were probably told it's a data server for the county or something. An inconvenience and an eyesore, but nothing exciting."

Mark had a lot of questions, but she held up a finger. "Hang on. I need to see if the other sites the robots broke in to also have these servers."

She was typing again, frenzied and frenetic, pieces of hair slipping out of her ponytail. He was certain her methods of searching for the info they needed wasn't legal, but he wasn't going to stop her. He would take any method they could utilize if it meant taking down Joaquin and saving the lives of other robots.

He started another pot of coffee in the kitchenette, having a feeling they would need it.

"Yes, I knew it. We're right." Jenna pushed back in her chair and spun to look at him.

"More servers?"

"Yes, one of the other sites had servers in the building like the art gallery. The other two were adjacent to remote government offices. Joaquin is trying to access something on these servers. I don't know what, but I have no doubt that's what he's doing."

Mark still had a lot of questions. He handed her a cup of coffee. "Are you sure? The door in the art studio wasn't breached—that bookshelf we moved hadn't been touched recently. And I've seen pictures of the other sites—there weren't any signs of trying to access an adjoining building in those. Pretty sure that would have been obvious."

"That's the thing, though." Jenna's eyes were fully alive and dancing with energy. Caught up in the solving of a mystery and not blaming herself for things that weren't her fault. Damned if he didn't love seeing her this way. "Actual physical access to those servers wouldn't be necessary. Joaquin would… Hang on."

She turned back and started typing on the computer again.

"RATs," she said a few minutes later.

Now Mark was even more confused. "Rodents?"

She smiled. "Remote Access Tools—hackers call them RATs. Joaquin's robots aren't computer geniuses—none of them would be able to hack into the government's main systems—but they have enough basic knowledge to install RATs on these remote servers."

"And the robots didn't have to get on the computers to place these…RATs?"

"Yep. That's why it's a hacker's friend. The key thing about the RATs is that you don't have to be on the computer itself or even in the same room, just in a general proximity. Once a RAT is set up, it can siphon data without being detected."

"This is one of the things you test for as a cybersecurity expert, isn't it?"

"Absolutely. RATs are generally pretty easy to identify and eradicate *if* you're looking for them. But I doubt the US government is actively protecting these servers. They think hiding them is enough."

"What sort of information leak are we talking about? What would Joaquin have access to?"

She spun to look at him again. "That, I'm not sure. I will dig deeper into each of the servers we know about, but undoubtedly there are more, and he's siphoning different pieces of information from each one."

He scrubbed a hand down his face. "Then, of course, he's making it look like a smash and grab so no one suspects what's really going on. There could be other break-ins we don't know about."

"I'm sure there are."

Mark stood. "I've got to call this in. I'm not sure how law

enforcement will want to tackle this, but Callum and Omega Sector definitely need to know all this, stat."

His phone was in his hand when it rang. Callum's name was on the screen as if Mark had summoned him. "Callum? We made a breakthrough, and you need to hear it."

"It'll have to wait for just a second," Callum said. "We have another robot. The victim is alive."

"Where?"

"Durango, Colorado. It will take just as long for you to drive as fly. It's three and a half hours to the north. I'm sending directions as we speak. I heard we lost the last one, but I'm hoping there's something that can be done to save this one."

"We're on our way."

Chapter 14

Jenna worked while Mark drove toward Colorado.

He would've liked her to sleep. The lack of rest—even for very good reasons like sinking into her soft body and driving them both crazy—wasn't helping either of their focus or energy. But Jenna was near buzzing with the need to help this newest robot, so Mark didn't press her to rest.

He knew what it was to push exhaustion to the side to complete a mission. He wouldn't rob her of that.

The hospital had already sent initial blood work from the robot for her to look at. She wouldn't be able to do full and true diagnostics until they arrived and she had the lab equipment she needed, but she was attempting to narrow down the effects of the tail based on what she'd learned from losing Brett Cochran.

"I need to focus on compounds that affect memory," Jenna said.

"Why do you think that?"

"It's what I would do if I were Joaquin. If you're going to leave a tail that affects a robot's health, might as well kill two birds with one stone by making it something that affects memory. That way, if a robot does survive, he or she won't remember anything."

"Smart. The robots couldn't provide any info about computers or let law enforcement know what was really happening."

"It's next level plausible deniability. They wouldn't be lying, they genuinely would have no memory of anything. They wouldn't be able to recall it even if someone put them into a hypnotic state."

He squeezed the steering wheel. "So the tail might serve multiple purposes: erasing the robots' memories and eliminating them altogether if they're caught. It would also keep the robots coming back to him for their *fix*."

"Maybe these are tests," Jenna said. "We only know about a few robots, but there are probably dozens. If some of the robots are able to get in and out of their location without detection, maybe he'll escalate to trying to do something that isn't masked by a break-in."

Mark could think of a thousand ways Joaquin could escalate his use of robots, and none of them was good.

Jenna fell quiet, and he heard the telltale sounds of her focusing and typing, following the leads from their discussion.

Thankfully, there wasn't any traffic on the way to Durango, so they'd made good time. Callum was on top of the logistics, for which Mark was grateful. Jenna needed to focus on saving the next victim's life, and Mark wanted his only focus to be on her.

He shifted, feeling a tingle in his leg.

Not now, he begged his body. He couldn't have a flare-up now. Jenna needed him to be in top form, end of story. That was what needed to happen. Not this bullshit he couldn't control.

Grinding his teeth, he focused on the road and getting to

the hospital once they reached Durango. This was a much smaller town than Albuquerque.

"We're definitely on the right track about Joaquin accessing computers. Callum just sent me the info about the latest robot's break-in. Bookstore this robot robbed is right next to a backup for the Department of Transportation."

Mark made a face. "Transportation. Why would he want access to that?"

"I'm not sure. None of these servers holds high-level data," Jenna said. "Maybe he's trying to gather information that might give him leverage for what he's really after. It's impossible to know."

Mark made a turn. "The DOT is in charge of all federal transportation projects and the safety regulations. If he wanted to cause havoc, that would certainly be one way to do it."

"True."

He could sabotage the construction of a bridge or cause problems in air traffic control safety. Mark didn't love the idea of even these lower-level agencies being breached, given the things they could affect.

Joaquin was cunning enough to realize that he didn't need to have his hands on a nuclear bomb to wreak havoc. Little bits of power collected over time could do plenty of damage as a whole.

Joaquin had to be stopped, and not just because of the people whose lives he was stealing then leaving for dead. He had to be stopped before he could complete whatever his bigger plan was.

"We're almost there," Mark told Jenna.

"Good." She sounded confident. "We're starting in a much better place this time."

Pulling up to the doors of the hospital, he was surprised to find Callum waiting there in the flesh.

"Callum is here."

"What?"

"He's standing outside. I don't know why. He didn't tell me he would be here."

"Okay." Her voice was tight.

He put the bus in park and turned to her. Jenna was standing, brushing invisible dirt off her clothes and shaking out her hands.

"Okay. Yeah. That's fine. We're close to the door, right?"

"We're very close. But Callum being here means nothing. I can carry you inside. It seems to help."

"It does help," she said quietly. "Being out there still makes me feel like I'm going to hurl my guts up, but it helps. But Callum can't see me like that." Immediately, she held out a hand to stop his protest. "I know you think I'm overreacting about people knowing, but I don't want people in my professional life to look at me like I'm a freak. Or that I can't handle something as mundane as a few steps to a door."

He wanted to grab her and pick her up anyway, but that wasn't how to handle this. And hell if he didn't understand the need to keep professional weaknesses secret. It wasn't like he was going around announcing his peripheral neuropathy to his colleagues.

He stopped the nervous movement of her hands. "For the record, I don't think you're overreacting. I would never think that. I don't think you need to hide what you're going through, but that's up to you."

She was still staring at the floor.

"If you want me to carry you, I'll do that. If you want me to walk in beside you, holding your hand, I'll do that. If you want me to stay in the bus and leave you alone…that's an option too. I'm here for what you need."

He slipped a hand behind her neck and lifted her eyes to his. "I don't like seeing you in pain, little librarian. But I meant what I said. I'm here for what you need me to do, even if that means watching you struggle for this piece of it."

She swallowed, eyes flickering all around like she couldn't focus because of her fear. "Thank you. I—" She pressed her lips together. "I know you're right, but I'm not ready. Can you… Can you distract him? I'll go straight in. I can make it. If you're talking to him, maybe he won't pay attention to me."

Mark grinned. "I don't think anyone would be able to not pay attention when you walk by."

She rolled her eyes but smiled the slightest bit. "Trying to secure your place in the bed tonight?"

"Trying to distract you a little. Is it working?"

"Maybe."

"I'll talk to him," he said. "I need to tell him what we talked about on the drive anyway. You can do this."

Jenna closed her eyes for a long moment, steadying herself. "Okay."

"Let's do this." He bent down and kissed her briefly then turned and went to the door of the bus, Jenna crowding right behind him. He punched in the door code and stepped down and out of her way, immediately focusing on Callum.

"Hey, Callum. I didn't expect you here in the flesh. Thought you were undercover."

He only felt the air behind him as Jenna sprinted for the doors. Callum looked after her, and Mark stepped to intervene. "Jenna wants to get in there and start. Worked on the drive up, and the faster she's in, the better chance she has."

Callum nodded. "Yeah, okay, that's smart. I wasn't going to come, but if there's any chance this robot can survive, I wanted to be able to talk to her personally. Especially in light of what you guys found about the computer stuff."

"Jenna is concerned that the chemical tail being left in the robots might also affect their memories."

Callum scrubbed a hand down his face. The man looked like he'd been awake for way too many hours. Mark knew the feeling.

"Why does she think that?"

"She said it was what she would do if she were working for Joaquin."

"Shit." Callum's shoulders slumped. He didn't try to dispute Jenna's argument. Both of them knew her expertise went well beyond theirs.

"Yeah, my feelings exactly. I'm going to go park this thing."

"Okay, I'll be inside."

Mark parked the bus away from the building and went inside, finding his way easily to the lab with help from the hospital staff.

Callum stood outside the lab, looking through the small window on the door.

"Everything okay?" Mark asked.

"You tell me." Callum didn't look away from the window. "Is there something I should know about Jenna?"

Shit. "Like what?"

"I made my way down here, and she was standing in the hallway, facing the wall, sucking in air like she'd just run a marathon."

Damn it. Mark should've insisted on carrying her in. At least that way, she wouldn't have had to battle a panic attack.

But he would keep Jenna's secret. "This is all hard on her. She feels responsible for the creation of these robots, and their deaths." No mention of fears or agoraphobia.

"Is she going to be able to handle this?" Callum stepped back from the door.

"She'll get it done. Just give her space."

He pushed the door open, and Jenna glanced up at him from the microscope she was looking into.

"Permission to come aboard?"

Her jaw was tight. "Just you. Callum already suspects I'm cuckoo for cocoa puffs."

"I told him the incident he witnessed was stress about helping the robots and he bought that, so it's okay. How are you feeling?"

"My hands are shaky, and I'm pretty sure it's a good thing I didn't eat too much before attempting my dash in here or it would've ended up all over the floor. But I'm handling it." She blew out a breath. "Better having you here with me."

"Good." Slowly, he moved closer. He didn't want to infringe on her space, and he wouldn't reveal their personal relationship to Callum, but Mark was glad his presence helped her.

"You don't want Callum in here?"

"No. He would just watch, waiting. No matter how fast I go, he'd want me to go faster, and—" She heaved in a breath. "It's just a little too familiar."

Because Adil Garrison had done the same thing. Pressure her until she couldn't give him what he wanted, and then he took her outside and destroyed her, piece by piece.

Mark gave her a smile. "You work at your speed. You're accomplishing more than anyone else, so your speed is fast enough."

"Let's hope." She looked down at the computer screen next to the microscope. "I'm not messing around this time. I'm working straight from the assumption that Joaquin doesn't want these robots to survive or remember anything. I've already applied a first potential compound to the blood work."

Mark watched as she worked, muttering at the screen in her normal fashion. He stepped outside the lab to provide Callum with all the details they'd discovered about the computer hacking. While the information was helpful, it didn't allow them to be proactive—evidently, these government backup servers were located all over the country.

Shutting them down wasn't an option; they contained too much info. Using their locations to stake out potential robot attacks wasn't an option either—there were just too many of them.

So they would still be working on the defensive, not where Mark liked to be. Callum would be going back undercover, this time focusing on what was on those servers Joaquin was attempting to access.

Callum went to make phone calls, and Mark went back into the lab. Nurses had once again been running steady streams of samples and data to Jenna. Mark had stayed nearby in case she'd needed him, but apparently once she'd recuperated from the panic attack, she'd found a way to steady herself.

Mark watched her from just inside the door. She was so focused, she didn't even see him there. It was so damned sexy. Her hair had half fallen out of her ponytail, and her glasses were so far down her nose they were in danger of sliding off. She'd rolled up the sleeves on the boxy white lab coat.

Damned if he didn't want to see her wearing that lab coat and nothing else. When this was all over, that was going to happen.

She straightened from whatever she'd been staring at on the screen. "Oh my God."

"What?"

There was pure relief in her eyes. "I think I have it this time. I think I can save her."

This robot was a young woman named Sarah, twenty-four, and just like yesterday, her body was failing, now dependent on drugs she hadn't been given. "Really?"

"It might take a couple of tries to get it right, but yeah. She's definitely responding."

Mark smiled. "I'm not going to because Callum is still nearby, but I need you to know that I want to kiss the shit out of you right now."

She blushed, punching buttons into the computer before looking over to make sure the machine was following her instructions. "Thank you for not, though I would enjoy it. It's not that I want to keep you a secret, I just—"

"You don't have to explain," he said gently. "I understand. Focus on what you're doing. The rest of it can come later."

She nodded and went back to work, dispatching a nurse with the mixture she'd just created. Once again, it didn't work, but Sarah wasn't getting worse. Three samples later, her vitals rose out of danger.

"I think this is it," Jenna said. "I think this will work. We'll have to monitor her and keep giving her this compound, and I'll tweak it if we need to, but if it's working, she should be awake within the hour."

Mark made sure the coast was clear before he pulled Jenna into a closet and kissed her thoroughly. It was hot, hard, and way too brief, but they were both smiling when they emerged, ready to monitor and wait.

Chapter 15

Mark was watching with Jenna when the robot woke up.

Not a robot… *Sarah*. She was a person now, no longer being controlled by Joaquin or anyone else.

She was confused and scared, but she was alive, and that was the important thing. Sheer relief shone in Jenna's eyes as she looked at Sarah from the doorway, then she excused herself to go back to the lab to run more tests and make notes for the doctors and nurses.

Mark and Callum stayed. Sarah needed to be questioned as soon as possible.

"When can I question her?" Callum asked a doctor as he stepped out of the room.

The doctor shook his head. "Not for a while. She's awake, but she's confused and scared."

"We won't do anything to cause her undue distress," Mark reassured the doctor. "But she may know things that are vital to national security."

"Right now, that young woman can't even remember her name, so I'm pretty sure details of national security are going to be beyond her grasp. Let us get her more stable and comfortable, then we can look into questioning. Her health is the most important thing."

Callum's jaw clenched. "How long do you think we're talking about?"

The doctor shook his head. "At least six hours. Twelve would be better."

They both nodded at the man, and he left.

Callum leaned back against the wall. "I can't afford to be away from my undercover assignment for another six to twelve hours. I'm risking too much just by being here now."

"Then go. I'll question Sarah as soon as it's possible. I'm closer to the situation anyway. I'll report any actionable intel immediately."

Callum still looked torn. And exhausted. He ran a hand through his already tousled hair. "You're doing a lot as it is, man. And we're not even paying you."

"Ian is paying me, so don't worry about that. You can't do it all, Callum. You being undercover probably does a lot more toward us shutting Joaquin down than sitting in this hospital does. I'll get you the info you need."

"If there's any to get," Callum responded. "Like Jenna said, Joaquin might have been smart enough to use drugs on his victims that affect their memory."

Mark reached up and squeezed Callum's shoulders. "Whatever intel there is to get from Sarah, I'll get it. You get back to where you're needed."

For a second, it looked like Callum might argue, but then he nodded. "Okay. Thank you. I wouldn't trust this to just anyone."

"I won't let you down."

~

Mark spent most of the day in the lab with Jenna. They were both carefully monitoring Sarah's progress. Mark could feel weariness, compounding the effects of his peripheral neuropathy, pulling at him, but he ignored it.

Jenna was exhausted also. "Damn it, this latest compound didn't have the desired result either. Honestly, Sarah's memory might be gone for good."

He came up behind her and rubbed her shoulders. "It's okay. She's alive, awake, and stable."

"But if you aren't able to question her…"

"Then I'm not able to question her. That's still secondary to the fact that she's not going to die in this hospital today."

She leaned her head back so it rested against his abdomen, closing her eyes. "I just wanted us to get the answers we need."

"We will. Maybe not with Sarah, but with the next robot. You made huge progress here today, librarian. How about we go get some sleep then you can try fresh in the morning?"

She bent her head and kissed the top of one of his hands that was rubbing her shoulder "Can I have a couple more hours? I have a few things I want to try that will take more time to work through Sarah's system to see if it has any effect."

He kissed the top of her head. "Sure. Do you want food? Coffee?" He'd already gotten them dinner a couple hours ago, but he didn't mind being the resident errand boy. If the roles were reversed, she would do the same.

"What I want is you," she whispered as the nurse who'd been in the lab exited. "Will you be my reward for working hard?"

"Oh, I think I can find plenty of ways to properly reward you." He bent down and nipped her ear just hard enough to make her squirm. "So hurry up and get your work done."

She giggled—damn well the most intriguing sound he'd

ever heard—and he sat down on a stool near the door so he'd be out of the way. He straightened out his right leg in front of him. It was dragging slightly again. His left hand was tingling also, an irritation that would eventually lead to pain, another sign his peripheral neuropathy was acting up.

He needed to rest. Needed to get back to the doctor and talk about possibilities—medications and electrical nerve stimulation treatments that may not stop what was happening to his body but would at least give options.

He was going to have to tell Jenna about this before too much longer. The whole truth.

But that could come after the case. After they stopped Joaquin.

Nurses and doctors came in and out of the lab to consult with Jenna. Mark had to hand it to them; none of them gave her grief about being in charge. Callum had run good interference for her, setting her up as the resident expert before she even arrived.

Then Jenna had completely proven him right.

Not to mention, she was great with the medical staff. It was good that no one else from Linear or Zodiac Tactical was here to see her. If they had been, her excuses for keeping them at arm's length because she just wasn't good at being around people would be shot to hell.

His leg twitched, and he decided to walk a little to stretch it out. He let Jenna know, not offended when she haphazardly raised a hand to signify she'd heard him when he announced what he was doing. He would go by Sarah's room to see if she happened to be up to talking.

He'd been by twice already today, talking to her briefly each time. He'd questioned her gently, but it didn't take long to realize she didn't remember anything.

Not just anything concerning Joaquin and what he'd done to her...she didn't remember anything about *anything*.

Not her name, age, favorite color…nothing. It was terrifying for the young woman, so he hadn't pressed. The doctor said her memories would either come back or they wouldn't.

Jenna said they wouldn't. This wasn't some head trauma causing amnesia. The chemical compounds Sarah had been given had probably erased her memories forever.

It was late evening now. Sarah was in a more isolated corner of the small hospital, so there weren't many people around. Mark glanced into her room as he walked by, glad to see she was sitting up and talking to a nurse.

He made a lap around the hospital, his leg not feeling better, but at least not feeling worse. As he passed Sarah's room the second time, a doctor was talking to her, a syringe in hand.

Mark kept going then stopped. He hadn't seen that doctor all day. Not that he'd seen every doctor in this hospital, but no one should be administering anything to Sarah without checking with Jenna first.

Maybe he'd just come on shift and didn't realize how complicated her case was. Mark stepped back into the doorway and entered the room.

"Excuse me." He used his best Southern drawl to try to put the doctor at ease. He wasn't trying to make life more difficult for anyone. "Not trying to tell you how to do your job, but have you checked to make sure whatever you're about to give Sarah won't affect the other tests being performed on her?"

"I've got this. Thanks."

Mark stepped farther into the room. "Look, maybe you're just coming on shift and—"

Mark broke off. Why was this doctor on the wrong side of Sarah's IV with a syringe in his hand? All medicines should be going through the IV, not poking her again unnecessarily.

Something wasn't right here.

Mark was already diving for him when the *doctor* brought the syringe up over Sarah's chest like it was a fucking knife.

He crashed into the man before he could succeed in filling her with whatever was in the syringe. The motion of his tackle brought them both down on top of poor Sarah, who started screaming. Mark cursed as the fake doc caught him with an elbow to the face, knocking him off the other side of the bed.

The perp ran out the door.

"Sarah, are you okay?"

Sarah was crying but nodded. Mark bolted into the hall after the perp, shouting for the nurses to call security and to get a real doctor to check on Sarah.

The fake doc was sprinting down the hallway. They were on the ground floor. Mark had to catch him before he reached the outside. The guy took a sharp turn down a hallway that circled around toward the back entrance.

Mark had been here long enough today to know his way around. He angled down a different hall that would allow him to cut the guy off at the entrance.

He pushed for as much speed as he could. The hospital staff looked at him like he was out of his mind, but he didn't slow down.

Then his leg started to drag.

Shit. Mark pushed down the anger at his own body's betrayal. He could make it. He had to catch this guy.

He burst through a door at the end of one hallway, his leg dragging further. Had he gotten there quickly enough? Slamming footsteps came from the other direction, and Mark moved, lunging out of sight so he could come at the guy sideways.

Moving at full speed, the fake doctor blew into the lobby, and Mark sprang. It felt like slow motion. He was on a collision course to take down the suspect who had no doubt just tried to kill Sarah…

And then Mark couldn't feel his leg at all.

It was nothing more than a stump attached to his body, and he had no control. He couldn't keep upright or maintain his momentum, crashing to the floor just behind the man. Mark didn't have time to catch himself, and he was a blend of numbness and pain as he hit the floor.

By the time he looked over, the man was gone, flying out the doors and into the Colorado evening.

The nurses who'd seen what happened rushed to help him, but he waved them off. He slammed his fist against the wall. Shame burned in his lungs and under his skin.

His body had failed him.

Grief came hard on the heels of the shame. This wasn't going to stop, and it wasn't going to get better.

He pushed those thoughts away.

"Call the police," he managed to tell the nurses. "And get a picture of his face from the cameras. He tried to kill someone."

Lauren Marino, Callum's Omega Sector colleague, came running from the other way. She stared at Mark on the floor. "You okay?"

"Yeah." Damn it, he still couldn't get up, but he wasn't going to explain that to her. "I think Joaquin sent someone to kill Sarah. He ran out the back exit."

"I'll call it in and get security footage and a guard placed on Sarah's door." She ran out the door the perp had gone through, phone already in hand.

A security guard offered Mark a hand up. His leg still wasn't in good shape, and it probably wouldn't be for a while. He braced himself on the reception desk for balance.

Lauren came back inside a few minutes later. "No sign of him out there."

"Sorry I wasn't able to stop him."

Her eyes narrowed. "You sure you're okay?"

He forced a smile. "Just not getting any younger."

She was young, fit, and had obviously never had her legs just stop working in the middle of a chase. Her smile was forced. "Yeah."

She got on her phone and called in the situation. As she walked down the hall, the last thing he heard her say was that the perp had escaped despite a foot chase with a Zodiac agent. That she didn't know how or why. Shit happened.

Mark slumped, using the counter for more support.

Shit happened.

And someone who might've been able to provide usable intel about Joaquin had gotten away. There was nothing Mark could do about it.

Right now, all he could do was wait until he could walk on his own again.

Chapter 16

Jenna stood at the entrance of the hospital, staring out at the bus that was parked about twenty yards away. She'd been here for way too long—people were starting to stare. A nurse asked if she was okay. A teenage candy striper asked if Jenna needed help calling an Uber and offered to explain how the app worked.

Jenna had managed not to roll her eyes or explain she could write those types of apps in her sleep.

But she didn't manage to force herself to make a dash for the bus.

The last couple hours had been chaotic. Three nurses had run into the lab and explained that an unauthorized man dressed like a doctor had entered Sarah's room. Evidently, he'd tried to inject her with something, but Mark had stopped him.

Jenna and the doctors had then needed to make sure the man hadn't done anything else to Sarah. Thankfully, her vitals were steady and blood work had come back clean—or at least clean for her, given all the compounds already being pushed into her system.

But someone had tried to kill her—the results of what had been in that syringe proved it. Jenna had no doubt the pretend doctor man was another one of Joaquin's robots. They hadn't captured him, but at least now law enforcement was standing guard outside Sarah's door. Nobody else would be getting to her.

Agent Marino had stopped by and let Jenna know there was a small government lab nearby that had given Jenna permission to continue to work so they weren't in the hospital's way. Tomorrow, that was where they would go. There wasn't anything else to do here, and the blood samples she needed would be sent to the other lab.

Jenna hadn't seen Mark since before the fake doctor incident. She'd texted him to let him know she was ready to leave if he was.

His response hadn't been what she was expecting.

Bus is out front as close as possible. I can't carry you tonight. I'm sorry. I'll explain.

So, here she was as she'd been for the past thirty minutes, staring at the vehicle like twenty yards was twenty miles away.

Logically, she knew if Mark wasn't able to carry her, there was a good reason. She couldn't doubt that, not after how attentive and understanding he'd been about all her quirks. She liked what was happening between them, and despite her nerves about letting anyone too close, Mark was getting under her skin.

And she didn't mind it. Not even a little bit.

He wouldn't have left her here to face this alone if there were other options.

Maybe he'd had to go to the police station or something. Maybe to meet Callum or do some other super-secret law enforcement stuff. Mark knew how hard getting to the bus would be for her.

He wouldn't just leave her here.

She had to go. She couldn't stand here all night. She grabbed her phone.

I'm about to make my getaway to the bus. It is unlocked, right?

The last thing she wanted to do was force herself out there, only to have to come back because a door was locked. But she might not have a choice. She wasn't sure if Mark could respond to a text right now. He may be too busy.

Yeah. I'm inside the bus. Door is unlocked.

She stared at the phone in her hand for a long minute. He was already inside the bus? She waited for him to offer to come get her.

But…nothing.

So much for not just leaving her here.

No way to delay the awful any longer. Mark wasn't here to carry her—literally or figuratively—so she had to do this herself. She pushed off the wall and walked out the door, knowing waiting would make the terror worse.

It was dark outside the hospital. The lights in the parking lot and under the portico were bright, but she could still see the black sky, and her whole body shuddered. The air was cool around her, which should feel good against her skin, but instead felt like sandpaper scraping her and rubbing her raw.

She could see the bus, but it seemed to get farther with every step, not closer. She sped up, the sound of her labored breath the only thing she could hear. Nausea curdled her stomach, and her vision dimmed. She kept her sights planted on the bus and kept moving forward.

By the time she made it to the door, she was staggering like a drunk person. She pulled it open and leaped inside. Mark caught her as he pressed the button to close the doors, but he went down, and she went with him.

It took her a minute to get the panic under control, for

her body and mind to realize she wasn't in any danger. Lying there, she rested on top of Mark, catching her breath.

Wait, why had they fallen? She hadn't realized she'd crashed into him so hard. "I'm sorry for bowling you over. Are you okay?"

He wrapped his arms tighter around her. "Are you okay? I'm so sorry you had to get back out here by yourself. I got the bus as close as I could, but…"

She pushed away from him and got up. "Yeah, I made it. Gotta learn to fend for myself, right?"

He let out a sigh. "No, little librarian, you shouldn't have had to fend for yourself. I should've been there to help you."

Why weren't you?

She wanted to shout it. Now that she was back inside her home base and feeling better by the second, she wanted to know why he'd abandoned her when he could've so easily been inside the hospital to at least help escort her out.

She wanted to know how she could've been so wrong about what was between the two of them. He obviously wasn't thinking of them as a team, a couple, or he never would've—

Why was he still on the floor?

"Are you okay?" she asked.

He sighed again. "I've been better."

"Is there a reason you're still on the floor?"

He rubbed a hand down his face. "Mostly because I don't want to look like some invalid in front of you."

Shit. She dropped back down beside him. "What happened? Where are you hurt? Did you get shot?" She started moving her hands around his body, looking for a wound. "They told me there was a bad guy, but they didn't tell me you'd gotten hurt. Why didn't you—"

He grabbed her roaming hands. "I didn't get hurt."

"Then what is going on?" There was some big piece of information she was missing.

"Do you mind helping me up? I got special permission for the bus to park here, but we need to move."

She nodded, still not understanding what was going on. She helped him up, watching him carefully. He was stiff and slow, but he didn't seem to have any specific wounds. She helped get him into the driver's seat then he fired up the bus.

She stood right behind him as he drove, trying to piece together anything she could. Mentally, he seemed fine, and nothing about his driving concerned her. They were both silent as he drove a few miles then parked inside a secure lot.

When the engine was off and all the security was in place, he stood. He was able to walk on his own back to the table, but he was limping.

"I thought you said you weren't wounded? Did you fall?" Dread spiraled through Jenna. "What's going on?"

He sat down, and she sat across from him.

His face looked haggard. "You know how I went down when we were sparring?"

She nodded.

"When I was a SEAL, I was injured. Multiple times. It's the nature of the job. Most of the time, everything turns out fine, but I got unlucky. I got hit in the spine one too many times and…" He sighed, shoulders sinking like the weight of the world was suddenly on them. "I have what's called peripheral neuropathy."

Her brain flew through what she knew about the condition. "Nerve damage."

"Yes. It comes in and out, mostly with my legs, but also my arms sometimes. I'll be fine for weeks at a time, and then out of nowhere, it fucks me. I was in the middle of tackling the guy who attacked Sarah when my leg went numb. I couldn't control it, couldn't stop it. And then he was gone."

His hands were on the table in front of him, folded into fists in anger. She didn't blame him. Having something hijack your life in a way that made you rage at the universe?

That was an experience she was familiar with.

"Does Ian know?"

"Yeah. I couldn't hide this from him—not when a client's safety could be jeopardized because of it. I've been trying to make it work as long as I can. But I can't protect people if my body is going to fail at a critical moment. Like what happened tonight."

"You know what some jackass said to me the other day?"

He raised an eyebrow. "What?"

"What you can do is all you can do."

He let out a low chuckle. "Yeah, that definitely sounds like a jackass."

She stood and went to the other side of the table, sliding onto the bench with him. "You did what you could."

He smiled, but it didn't reach his eyes. "Now I know how it feels to be on the other end of that advice. It doesn't really help, does it?"

"No, it doesn't." She slipped her hand into one of his. "What do the doctors say? Is it going to get better?"

"Fully? No. And there's no way to tell how bad it will get, and in my line of work, inconsistency isn't something I can live with. So, it looks like I'll be moving to a desk job."

She let out an exaggerated gasp. "Sitting at a desk and accomplishing important things? No! Anything but that."

"I know, I know. You do it all the time. But I'm not a desk person."

"Maybe your new normal won't have to be at a desk. There has to be something in between Mission: Impossible-type shenanigans and sitting all day, every day in a job you hate."

"Maybe."

He didn't believe her, but Jenna knew she was right. Between her, the Zodiac team, and the Linear Tactical guys, they would find something for him. And not just busywork. Her Outlaw was too important to relegate to something that made him feel trivial.

Her Outlaw.

How many times over the past few days—and even before—had he shown her she didn't have to face things alone?

Now it was her turn to show him.

"Are you in pain right now?" Jenna asked him.

"No. I'm stiff and clumsy, but no real pain."

Good. She didn't want him to be in pain. But she wanted him.

But first, she wanted him to know she understood.

She moved, straddling his hips so they were face-to-face. With a conversation as intimate as this, she wanted to be touching him.

"When I was taken, I was changed," she said quietly, settling her arms around his neck as his hands landed on her hips. "My entire life was stolen from me. You've seen it. And as much as I like to think someday I'll be able to just…stand outside and feel the wind in my hair and the sun on my skin again, I don't know if it'll ever happen. What Garrison did changed me so deeply, I get angry every fucking day."

His brows creased and he nodded. She could see the anger he was also feeling on her behalf.

But this wasn't about her.

"And you're the same," she continued. "It's not happening as quickly to you, but your life as you knew it has also been stolen. You have to watch it happen in slow motion and know it's happening. I can't even imagine that. I'm not sure which way is worse."

He leaned his forehead against hers, sliding his hands up her ribs. "I think they're both equally bad in different ways. But I've never thought of the comparison before."

She smiled and winked at him. "I don't know if you knew, but I'm brilliant. So you should always believe everything I say."

He chuckled. "Oh, I definitely know you're brilliant, little librarian."

She cupped his cheeks. "You will find a way to survive this new normal. I may not be such a hot example of doing that, but it is possible. You find a way to exist, to thrive even. You can do that, Outlaw."

His mouth was on hers before she even finished the sentence. No words passed between them for long minutes, both of them getting lost in each other. Mark broke their kiss just long enough to continue the trail along her jaw. "We should eat something. You've been working hard all day."

"Later," she murmured. Food was the last thing on her mind right now. "You comforted me last night when I needed it, and I think, this time, you should take some comfort from me."

"Believe me," he said into the hollow of her throat, "it was far more than just comfort for me. I hope you know that."

"I do. It's—" Her breath hiccupped as he nipped at her skin. "It's scary, but I do."

"You don't have to be afraid of me, Jenna." He slid to the edge of the bench and let her stand, slowly backing her down the hallway to the bus's bedroom. His limp was hardly noticeable.

"Don't I?" Her words were barely a breath, and when her legs hit the bed, she fell back onto it, welcoming Mark's weight as he followed her down. "You're not going to steal my life, but you are going to change it. I don't know if I'm ready."

Mark took her hands and wove their fingers together, pinning her hands to the bed with gentle strength. "I'm not rushing you. But I'm not going to pretend I don't want you, and I'm not going to hide the fact that I'm playing for keeps. You're who I want, Jenna Franklin."

Emotion welled up in her chest. "Why? Why would you want me when I'm like this?"

He smiled. "You said it yourself. We're both our own kinds of broken. If you want to dig a cave to the center of the world and live there, I'll dig it myself and paint you a goddamn beautiful sky."

Everything in her body swooned. He meant every word he said, and it was as exhilarating as it was terrifying. Like going on a roller coaster without a seat belt.

He began kissing his way down her body over her clothes. "Tell me what you like."

She was embarrassed to say it, even after they'd already been together. "I don't want you to think differently of me."

His eyebrows rose into his hairline. "Unless you're about to confess to being a black widow and that you're planning to kill me after we have sex, that's not going to happen."

"I just—"

He caught her lips again, kissing them open and deepening the connection between both of them until she was breathless and arching beneath him. "Talk to me, Jenna. You've trusted me with so much else, trust me with this too."

This was the last piece of her, and it was harder than it should have been to let it go. Mark hadn't judged her about any of it—about the fear or her regression, about throwing up after stepping into fresh air. She took a deep breath and flexed her hands where they were still pinned to the bed by his.

"I like this," she whispered. "Rougher. Push and pull. Manhandling isn't out of the question." She looked at him. "As long as that's not hurting you."

Mark smiled. "Why did telling me that make you nervous?"

"Because I've been kidnapped," she said quietly. "I don't want people to think the two are connected. Or like… I don't know. Like I suddenly developed a taste for it after everything else."

His eyes darkened. "Even if that were the case, I wouldn't judge you for it."

He sank down her body, and she reached to stop him. The look he shot her now wasn't dark with anger or frustration on her behalf—it was filled with heat. "Don't move, Jenna."

His words—the deep timbre of his voice in that controlling tone—made her insides clench in the best way possible. "You don't have to do this."

"I'm well aware. That doesn't mean I'm not going to or that I don't want to."

Mark curled his fingers into the waistband of her pants and pulled them off. Already, she felt the difference between the tender comfort he'd shown her the night before and the unyielding command now. It drove heat straight into her in an entirely different way, along with the strong grip moving her thighs apart.

If anyone had told her the sight of Mark Outlawson with an arrogant smirk on his face while he knelt between her legs would be enough to undo her, she wouldn't have believed them. But it was true. A deep shudder of arousal rippled through her body.

He never broke her gaze as he stripped her underwear away. "Promise me one thing," he said.

"What's that?"

"If it's too much, or there's something you don't like, you'll tell me to stop. There's nothing offensive about that. I just need to be sure."

"I promise." But at the moment, there wasn't anything she could imagine him doing that would cool the heat raging within her.

"Good." Mark stood, no limp now, and flipped her with strong hands so she was on her knees. It was the only warning she had before his mouth was on her, consuming her from behind.

This wasn't slow, and it wasn't gentle. It was possession with lips and teeth and tongue, and she was deliciously help-less against it. Against him. More than anything—what she hadn't been able to truly put words to—she was broken enough already, so she didn't want anyone treating her like she was broken in the bedroom.

Pleasure spiraled through her, growing almost too fast. She moved, and Mark's hands landed on her hips, holding her exactly where he wanted her so he could push deeper with his tongue.

The shock of it was so unexpected, the heat pushed her over into a free fall of pleasure, flattening her down on the bed because her limbs were weak with the force of the orgasm.

No one she'd ever been with had gotten her to that point so quickly and thoroughly, and she didn't know if it was simply both of them being open and vulnerable with each other or if it was him.

Both. She hoped it was both.

Behind her, she heard the sounds of clothes coming off and a condom being put on before she felt him lifting her back onto her knees and helping her out of the rest of her clothes.

He roamed his hands up her body, touching her everywhere. No hesitation and no holding back. There was no glass doll here, and the relief she felt was only second to the sheer lust sliding over her like he was painting her with his fingers.

He flipped her again, dropping her on her back with amusement in his green eyes. Push and pull. When she ran a hand through his hair, he grabbed her wrist to yank her closer and kiss her with the same mouth that had just drowned her with pleasure. When she pushed him away playfully, he followed, nipping her lip to keep her close.

All at once, he lifted her knees, pushing them to her shoulders so he could enter her. And enter her he did, slamming home hard enough they both groaned.

"Outlaw," she breathed. "My Outlaw."

He was looking at her like she was the only thing that existed in the world, and she loved it.

He drove into her with hard, forceful strokes that felt like a claiming. Just feral enough to make her gasp, and tender enough to make her moan. It was everything, and she was lost in it.

They rose to pleasure together until all that was left between them were shaking breaths and unsaid words.

Mark lowered his forehead to hers for long moments before kissing her gently. It felt like there should be words to fill the silence, but neither of them was ready for that yet.

Finally, when they both had caught their breath, Mark pulled himself away to the bathroom to clean up, and Jenna found his shirt and put it on, enjoying the comfort of having the smell of him around her, just like last time.

He froze coming out of the bathroom. "If you ever want to eat tonight, I'm not sure wearing my shirt is the best idea."

"Why?" she teased, standing up from the bed and slipping past him to the food. "Like what you see?"

"You have no fucking idea," he muttered.

Jenna laughed and started putting together a plate of food to warm up. "Food first. Then, we'll see."

He grabbed his pants off the floor, and Jenna was fully aware that his eyes never left her. "Yes, we will see."

His voice left tingles on her skin, and she found herself eager to finish dinner.

Chapter 17

They got sleep.

Granted, their limbs were intertwined the whole night and Jenna woke up at dawn to the feel of Mark's lips making their way down her neck, which led to…*not* sleeping, but mostly, they got the rest they needed. At least, more than Jenna normally did.

Something had changed between them. Not just the sex, although that was amazing enough, but in the intimacy between them. She realized it as she lay in the bed with him —his face buried in her neck, leg hiked up over her hips— running her fingers through his thick brown hair. This newfound intimacy was less about physical closeness and more about there being no more secrets between them.

He knew her weaknesses, and she knew his.

She hated to hear about his peripheral neuropathy because she knew how heavy that weighed on him. He was going to have to change damned near everything about his life.

But he could do it. He was smart and resilient enough to adapt. Where some people might let hopelessness and depression cloud everything with this new condition, Outlaw would persevere. It was the core of his nature.

And she hoped he would let her help him walk through this. That maybe in some way, all their jagged parts would fit together to make some sort of beautiful whole.

The morning between them was quiet and comfortable. They both had work to do—Mark trying to help identify the man who'd tried to kill Sarah, and Jenna working on further compounds to see if they could help the woman regain her memory.

After lunch, they headed over to the county lab. It was much better equipped than the hospital—the kind of lab Jenna would have set up for herself if she were interested in doing this work full time. Well, maybe it didn't have every bell and whistle, but she was content with what she had. This would allow her to make good progress.

She wanted to be ready for when the next robot was found.

Part of that was through trying to help Sarah regain her memories. Even if the memories the woman recovered weren't helpful in taking down Joaquin, Jenna wanted to give her back as much of her life as possible.

Just because the sequence Joaquin's bioengineers created had caused Sarah's brain to short-circuit and dissolve her memories didn't mean the memories were no longer there. It was harder than one imagined to fully wipe someone's memory.

The easiest solution was to create some sort of mental work-around. To come at the memories from a different angle. Sarah's brain still stored all the info; Jenna needed to figure out a way to trick her system into accessing it.

Hopefully, once Jenna did that, it would be possible to immediately reverse effects on future robots.

If Jenna could actually do it.

She *would*. She had helped start this nightmare, and she would help end it. Now, it was a question of doing it before the next robot was found.

As she worked all afternoon and into the evening, Mark sat at a computer on the other side of the lab going through a very sensitive database of the secret government backup servers. He was trying to piece together where Joaquin might send the next robot or any kind of clue about what that bastard was ultimately trying to do.

Through the hours, she'd been sneaking glances at him. He'd been doing the same to her. She couldn't remember the last time she'd felt like this. Giddy and light-headed and distracted, despite the importance of her work.

"Well," Mark said. "Shit."

"What?"

He shook his head. "The server search is too broad. They're all over the country. Without knowing what intel Joaquin is trying to get from them, it's too many to narrow down."

Jenna input another sample compound and set it to run. She needed to wait for the results, so she walked over to him. "We know two were the Department of Transportation and the IRS. What was the first one?"

Mark checked. "FEMA."

"That doesn't seem to make sense. Those aren't the agencies you'd expect Joaquin to dig into."

"So, a dead end." Mark leaned back in his seat. "Yet another one. They weren't able to find the guy who tried to attack Sarah either."

He still felt guilty about letting the man get away. Omega Sector agents had been looking along with the local police, but it was as if he disappeared into thin air. It wasn't surprising if he was under the same chemical subjectification as the other robots. The programming would tell him where to go, make him stronger and faster and not let him stop until he was where he needed to be or died.

The syringe he'd tried to inject Sarah with had contained poison that would have killed her in minutes. Whatever Joaquin was doing, he very much didn't want it getting out.

Jenna rubbed Mark's shoulders. "If it helps, even if you would've caught him, he probably still wouldn't have been able to tell us anything. He'd be under the same chemical and genetic modifications as Sarah and the other robots."

"I'd like to know that for sure, rather than just assume." He spun in his chair and reached for her, tugging her closer by her belt. "It's late. Should we start again tomorrow?"

There was a playful glimmer in his eyes that told her exactly what he was thinking, and she was fully on board. "Let me just finish this one test," she said. "Then I'll be ready."

She still felt the pressure to get this work done, but with no one currently in danger, she could take another night to try to get a decent amount of sleep.

And...*other stuff*.

The computer was still running the sample, and it would take a while. She set it up so the results would be sent to the bus. "Okay, I've got it so the results will be sent to me. I can check them later. I'm ready whenever—"

Mark was suddenly behind her, backing her against the lab table. "I'm ready." He pressed against her. "It seems like with you, I'm always ready."

She didn't even try to stop the catch in her breath at feeling him so close. "I like the sound of that. Let's get back home."

Home. The bus wasn't a home, but—

They both jerked slightly at a crashing sound outside. Both of them startled, pushing apart.

"What was that?" she squeaked.

Mark spun, putting himself between her and whatever danger there might be. She was about to explain it was probably something that had fallen, when the window to the front door of the lab shattered. A smoking canister flew through the broken pane, and Mark cursed.

"Come on, we've got to go. Back door."

He grabbed her hand, and they ran, the gas already filling the room by the time they made it to the back door that went into the hallway.

Jenna let out a gasp when she saw a man on the other side of the glass, his eyes empty, gun in hand. A robot.

Mark shoved the door outward and into him, knocking him over. The gun in the guy's hand went flying, Mark grabbed for it and clocked him over the head to keep him down without killing him.

Another man came running down the hallway at Jenna. Mark spun, catching the guy with a roundhouse kick that knocked him to the floor.

No sign of Mark's peripheral neuropathy right now, that was for damned sure

He didn't stop to celebrate; he grabbed her hand and started running down the hall. "Come on. I'm sure there will be more soon."

"They were robots."

"I know." Mark didn't slow down. "That's why I'm sure there will be a lot more."

She stopped short at the end of the hallway when they reached a door and she realized where they were going. *Outside*. Fear blanketed her mind, and her vision narrowed. Bile was already building at the base of her throat.

"Jenna." Mark squeezed her hand. "We have to go."

"I can't."

"It's the only way."

She yanked her hand out of his. "Mark, I can't go out there."

He took her face in his hands. Smoke was pouring through the hallway now, making it difficult to breathe. "Jenna, they are coming to take us, or maybe kill us outright. They're going to wait until they think we're passed out, then every single robot Joaquin sent will be coming in here to get us. We. Have. To. Go. It's the only way."

She couldn't do it. She just couldn't. "Mark—"

"I am going to be with you every fucking second, understand me? I know. I know what this will do to you, sweetheart, and I'm sorry. But I won't let you die."

Right now, dying by a quick bullet seemed better than trying to step foot out that door.

"Leave me," she whispered.

"There is not one goddamned way in hell I'm leaving you." He looked down at the gun in his hand, taking out the magazine then reloading it. He shook his head but didn't say anything.

He was going to stay. He was going to stay and try to shoot it out, even knowing the odds were total shit. Because of her.

It was one thing to be willing to die because of her fear. It was something else entirely to be willing to let Mark die with her.

Not to mention, it would be robots coming after them. Innocent people being used against their will that Mark would be forced to kill.

She had to go. But her muscles were frozen. She knew they only had seconds, and she still couldn't move.

She grabbed his wrists, digging her nails into his skin. "I don't know if I can go out there. I mean, I don't know if I can physically make myself do it."

Behind them came another sound of breaking glass. They were out of time.

"Do you trust me?"

"Yes," she gasped.

He kissed her on the forehead. "Close your eyes, little librarian."

Shouts sounded from behind them, and Mark didn't give her a choice. He grabbed her hand and opened the door, yanking her into the open air.

Immediately, the fear blazed through her mind like a flash of fireworks. She opened her eyes but still couldn't see, the empty, vast space around her about to swallow her up.

The lab was on the edge of town, intentionally far away from everything else. "We can't get to the bus," Mark muttered. "If the robots are smart, they will have blocked it off."

They ran. She had no idea where they were going. She was stumbling along behind Mark, letting him pull her toward the sparse pine trees that were scattered in front of them.

Trees.

Bark scratching against her skin.

Bright yellow eyes in the darkness.

Howling wind and freezing cold.

She stopped running and yanked her hand from Mark's, putting her hands over her ears in an effort to shut out the voice in mind. It didn't help. She couldn't breathe.

She heard a gunshot from behind them but couldn't escape her own nightmare enough to care.

"Get to the trees!" Mark shouted, pushing her forward with a hand on her back. He pulled up his gun to fire and let loose three shots before he was with her again. She'd barely been able to make it five steps without him.

The very air was weighing her down. Everything was

dark. The streetlights were behind them now, and in the trees were only shadows and the barest hint of moonlight.

She couldn't move any farther.

Mark wrapped an arm around her and yanked her against his chest. He somehow walked, protecting her with his body, while firing back another round at their pursuers. He pinned her to him, dragging her deeper into the woods. Her mind was shut down, and only fear remained.

She was going to die. Garrison would really win his bet this time. She would be dead by morning, and he would find her body half eaten and broken. Then he'd kidnap someone else to do his dirty work.

A whimper came out of her mouth as Mark pushed her against another tree, holding her there with his body. "Stay with me," he murmured. "You can do this, Jenna. Stay with me."

Why was Mark here? The flash of confusion in her brain rocketed her back to the present where there was nothing but adrenaline and pain, every nerve firing too rapidly, wretched, aching tingles crawling over her skin like live wires.

Mark stepped away and fired his gun, emptying the magazine before once again yanking her against his chest and moving them. They were in the dark, but she could hear the men coming for them.

More importantly, she could hear *Mark*. He was here with her. She had to keep the past and present separated, or she and Mark were both going to die.

"I'm out of ammo," he said. "Hiding is our only option."

She clutched at his chest and shoulders, trying to remain focused on the present and not let the past drag her under. Mark was here with her.

Mark was here. She repeated it in her mind like a mantra.

He kissed her on her forehead. "Keep quiet." He pressed

her face into his chest then wrapped his arms around her, pulling her deeper into the trees, then crouched down behind one. "Hopefully they'll think we kept running. We'll be okay."

But they both knew the chances of that happening were slim to none. Jenna kept herself pinned against Mark, trying to think through the panic and help him find a way out of this.

They were here for her. They wanted her alive. If they wanted them dead, they would've just blown up the whole building or something.

"They're after me," she whispered. "I-I can surrender, and you can run—"

Mark yanked her closer. "Not going to happen."

"But—"

New gunshots rang out behind them, along with the sounds of shouting. Jenna tensed, shuddering against Mark's chest, but he actually relaxed.

"Holy shit," Mark whispered. "I can't believe it."

She wasn't going to let him die. Finding a strength she didn't know she had, she pushed away from him.

"I'm going to surrender." Her stomach heaved and dizziness assailed her, but she meant it.

He kissed her hard on the mouth. "I appreciate the offer of protection, librarian warrior, but don't sacrifice yourself just yet. I think we have help on our side."

"How?"

"Hell if I know. But I'll take it."

Mark held her tightly, his arms and body wrapped so tightly around her that the noise from the firefight seemed distant. She heard some shouting then a loud series of shots all at once.

Then, nothing.

"Outlaw?"

Mark loosened his arms from around her just a little. "Over here, Aries."

Aries? That was Ian DeRose's code name. How had he known where they were or that they were in trouble? Those were the only thoughts her brain allowed before she spun to the side and heaved her guts up all over the pine needles.

Mark waited until she was finished to swing her up into his arms. Jenna closed her eyes and curled into him, not strong enough to pretend she could walk back on her own.

"You guys okay?" Ian asked.

"We're not hurt, but…I need to get Jenna back on the bus, stat, boss."

"You're clear. Sarge is out there. Landon too. No bad guys."

Jenna couldn't make sense of why Zodiac's top agents were here in the woods with them. But she didn't care.

"You took out the robots?" Mark asked.

"No, they all killed themselves when it became obvious they were going to be captured. We'll handle the scene. You take care of Jenna."

Mark was moving fast. Someone else said something to him—Sarge, maybe?—but he didn't stop. Jenna could barely hear anything over the sound of her own labored breaths, even though her body wasn't physically exerting itself in any way.

She tried to focus on him, on the smell of his skin against her face, on five things she could see or any other grounding exercise. But she couldn't hang on. Her mind was shutting down.

She heard the vague beeps of the bus's door code being pressed and knew she was almost to safety, but it was too late. Her body couldn't take any more.

"I'm sorry," she whispered.

"What? Stay with me, librarian." His arms tightened around her.

But she couldn't. Everything faded to pinpricks then black.

Then there was nothing.

Chapter 18

Jenna was a dead weight in his arms.

He carried her onto the bus and laid her on the bed. He felt for her pulse—it was still rapid, but steady. She wouldn't be out long.

Hell, it was a miracle she'd stayed conscious as long as she had.

A couple times out there, he'd been ready for her to lose it. Was ready to catch her and throw her over his shoulder if she passed out so they could keep going.

Or start screaming. He was beyond thankful her whimpering hadn't grown to more than that. But God, how it had shattered his heart to pieces to see and hear her that way.

And then for her to have offered to give herself up to save him... Not that he was going to allow that. He would've knocked her out cold himself first.

He brushed her hair back as her eyes began to flutter, and her breathing became more labored.

"You're okay, little librarian. Open your eyes. You're safe."

"Mark?"

"We're back in the bus, not outside. It's over."

Those brown eyes blinked open. "I passed out."

"You held on for a long time—handled the whole situation amazingly."

"It doesn't feel that way."

He kissed her forehead. "You held it together, that's what matters. We're both alive."

"Did I imagine Ian?"

"No, he and the Zodiac team showed up. I don't know how or why, but I'm thankful. I'm sure Ian will be here in a minute. Do you want to be alone? I can leave to debrief with him."

"No." Her whisper was desperate, and she wrapped an arm around his ribs, locking them together. He stroked her spine, savoring the feeling of her slowly relaxing and bouncing back.

Savoring the fact that she wanted him here with her. Especially since there was nowhere else on the planet he would rather be.

He was falling in love with this woman. Everything about her. Her intelligence and her bravery. Her beauty and the way she smiled. The way her fingers were digging into the back of his shirt right now, keeping him close.

He didn't care about her fear; all he cared about was that he could help make it better.

"Thank you," she said. "For getting me out of there. Even though—"

"I'll always get you out," he said. "No matter what I have to do, no matter what my body is doing, or yours. If you need me, I will get you out or die trying."

Her eyes went wide, like she could sense the true meaning behind his words, but she didn't back away or tell him it was too much. She just searched his face, then pulled him close.

A knock at the door of the bus had them pulling away. Jenna's breathing became rapid again.

Mark sat up. "We're safe. It's locked. It's probably Ian."

"Right," she said, blowing out a breath. "Right."

"I'll go out and talk to him. You stay here and rest."

"No," she said. "I'll be okay. Let him in. Give me a second to change clothes and brush my teeth, and then I'll come out."

Mark kissed her forehead then headed out to the front of the vehicle, closing the bedroom door behind him. He flipped on the monitor first to double-check it was Ian, then opened the door.

"Anybody else coming in?"

Ian shook his head. "Sarge and Landon are dealing with the bodies and law enforcement."

Ian stepped inside, and Mark sealed the door behind him, entering the security code.

Ian's face was hard. "You two all right?"

Mark nodded. "Jenna is pulling herself together in the bedroom. She'll be out…whenever she's ready."

Ian nodded. "Getting shot at is pretty fucking nerve-wracking."

"Yes, it is." If that's what Ian thought was the sole cause of Jenna's current recovery, so be it. Mark wasn't going to give up her secrets.

"Her agoraphobia probably made it a million times worse."

Mark kept his face neutral. "I'm not sure what you're talking about."

Ian sat down at the small table. "It's my business to know my employees—their strengths, weaknesses, and pressure points. I don't know the exacts about Jenna's fear of going outside, but I know it's a shit-ton more than her I-don't-like-to-be-around-people spiel."

Mark sat down in the booth across from him. "That information is Jenna's to share or not share."

"Fair enough," Ian said.

"How did you know we were in trouble? You arrived literally in the nick of time."

"Callum. He realized Joaquin was sending an entire slew of robots and figured out Jenna was the target. He couldn't get a call out without getting himself killed, but he sent an encoded message to our office."

"Jesus. How'd you guys get here so fast?"

"We were already on our way. Callum wanted you to have backup since it looked like things were starting to get messy. Sarge and I both are invested in taking down Joaquin before he can do his mind-control shit on anyone else, so we decided to come ourselves."

Both men had nearly lost the women they loved because of similar circumstances, so Mark wasn't surprised.

"Joaquin has got to be stopped. The people after Jenna and me tonight…"

"Robots, I know. Now, dead robots. At least six of them."

Mark knew they would've killed him without a thought to get to Jenna, but still…these weren't trained killers who had chosen to be on Joaquin's side. These were innocent people who'd had their choices stripped away from them. And now they were dead.

He heard the door to the bedroom click open, and a few seconds later, Jenna slid into the booth beside him. She still looked pale and gaunt, and her eyes were darting around everywhere. Her hands exhibited a fine tremor.

Her body was still barely out of panic mode. It would take a while for her subconscious to accept she was safe. There wasn't much Mark could do to help with that except be there for her. He slipped an arm around her shoulder and pulled her close, grateful when she cuddled in next to him.

"Hey, Jenna." Ian's voice was gentle. "You okay?"

She gave a one-shouldered shrug. "Better than I would've been if you hadn't shown up."

Jenna listened, tucked into Mark's side, as Ian explained again what had happened—the message from Callum all the way through to the dead robots. He was just finishing when he got a call from Callum. Ian put it on speakerphone.

"We got them in time, Callum," Ian said as he answered, bypassing any pleasantries. "I'm here with Jenna and Mark now."

"Sounds like we owe you one, Callum. Ian and the team showed up like the damned cavalry," Mark said. "We would've been in real trouble otherwise."

"We got lucky that I got word of the attack. Sorry I wasn't able to contact you directly. I was too busy saving my own ass. I'm out. They're going to know it was me who tipped you off."

"Shit." Mark rubbed his eyes. "Sorry, man."

"Don't be. It was worth it. I probably got as much as I could anyway. From what we've been able to piece together, Joaquin is siphoning data. Thanks to you figuring out he's using RATs, Jenna, we've been able to map at least some of the data he's accessed."

"Any results?" Jenna asked. Her voice sounded strained, probably from the vomiting.

"Yeah, and it's not good. Looks like he's orchestrating a major terrorist attack."

Jenna sucked in a breath. "Let me guess. He's aiming for something transportation-related, and maybe wants to cripple FEMA to make it worse?"

"It's looking that way. We don't have enough information to piece together the where or the how, but we'll keep digging."

"We're still having to play defense," Mark said. "I'd like

for us to get to a place where we can get ahead of Joaquin. Put him on the defensive."

"I think we all want that," Callum responded. "Jenna figured out how to combat the tail. That definitely gives us a leg up."

"Not much of one if he's got the robots programmed to kill themselves rather than be captured," Ian said. "Six dead."

Jenna sat up straighter. "Even worse, Joaquin's scientists can change the tail and we'll be back at square one with any new robots. Time will be critical for each."

Ian looked down at his phone as it buzzed. "Then we need to get ready to roll. Looks like we've had another B&E, another robot who's in the hospital and deteriorating fast."

Jenna was already scooting out from the table. "I have to send the hospital what they need to stabilize the victim." She looked over at Ian. "And I'd like to go, see if we can help the victim remember anything this time."

Ian nodded. "San Diego."

Jenna's face fell. "That'll take too long for us to drive."

"Already covered. I've got a plane ready that can transport the bus and us. It'll only take a couple of hours."

"Good. I'll get the info and start talking with the hospital staff." She rushed over to her computer and began typing.

"Where was the break-in?" Mark asked. "More specifically, what government server did it give them access to?"

Ian read the report on his phone. "FAA backup."

All of them went silent. If Joaquin had access to the FAA, he could cause all sorts of crises with air travel.

"The intel on that server shouldn't be critical info. None of them should contain critical info," Callum said.

Mark crossed his arms over his chest. "The pieces themselves aren't critical, but when they're all put together, the whole will equal something we won't like. I can basically guarantee it."

Neither of the other men argued.

"We have to work it one bit at a time. Let's get Jenna to this latest robot and see what we can find." Ian met Mark's eyes. "Is she going to be okay? Tonight was rough."

She wasn't listening to them; she was already on a video call with the doctor at the hospital. But she still looked frail, a little weak.

"She'll keep it together," Mark said. "She's stronger than she gives herself credit for."

"I'll meet you guys in San Diego." Callum disconnected the call.

Ian stood. "I'll go let Sarge and Landon know what's going on."

Mark grabbed his arm as he scooted by. "Thank you for finding a way to bring the bus with us."

Ian nodded. "Like I said, knowing my team's strengths and weaknesses makes me a more effective leader." He grinned. "Besides, what's the point in being a billionaire if you can't have toys?"

Mark shook his hand. "See you on the plane, Aries."

He exited as well, and Jenna and Mark stared at each other. She sighed with a tired smile. "Time for another adventure?"

"Can't wait." Grabbing the keys, he started the bus, and they headed out.

Chapter 19

They were able to drive the bus right up to the modified cargo plane at the small regional airport. From there, Jenna let Mark carry her up the outer stairs into the passenger section of the plane, too exhausted to care what Ian thought about it.

Mark left her inside briefly to help the loading staff with the bus, because neither of them wanted anyone else inside it.

Ian was already on board, head bent over a computer screen, talking to someone in a low voice on his phone. Jenna knew she should probably see if he needed any help, but she was tired enough she didn't want to engage yet. If she could maybe get some sleep on the plane, it would be good.

She smiled to herself. She couldn't remember the last time she'd looked forward to sleeping—forcing herself to rest had been a daily struggle since her captivity. But she wanted Mark with her. Mark soothed her mind in a way she couldn't fully explain. Almost as if her deepest subconscious knew he would keep her safe and let her relax.

He boarded the plane, and his eyes found her immediately.

No matter what I have to do… If you need me, I will get you out or die trying.

What he'd said to her in the bus… The words had been bouncing around in her head ever since. She kept waiting for them to terrify her, but they didn't. The opposite.

At the same time, thinking about the future, she didn't know how it would work. Her limitations weren't exactly conducive to a relationship or a family. How would he feel about that? How would *she* feel about that?

She pulled her thoughts back from that path, not having the energy to fully probe all of those questions.

Mark went over to stand by Ian. "Is there anything we need to know? Otherwise, I think Jenna getting some rest is the best thing we can do for this operation. She'll be working nonstop once we get to San Diego."

"Agreed," Ian said. "Just FYI, newest robot is female. She's already stable and recovering, thanks to Jenna's info."

That was one thing, at least. Joaquin hadn't changed the tail yet, so this victim would live.

"I will focus on memory recovery." She hated how scratchy her voice still sounded and how weak her limbs felt even now, hours later. "We're getting to her earlier in the process, so hopefully some of her memories will be recoverable."

Ian nodded. "You'll have a lab and access to everything you need. But yes, get rest now."

She walked back to the furthermost seats, which reclined flat. She sighed as she was able to stretch out.

Mark sat down next to her but didn't recline his connected seat.

"Aren't you going to sleep?" she asked. She wanted him sleeping beside her.

"I want to, but if I do what I really want—which is wrap you in my arms so both of us get better rest—Ian's going to know about us. I want to make sure that's okay."

"I'm too tired to care," she said, reaching over and taking his hand. "And…I don't care if Ian knows."

She didn't know how things would play out for her and Mark long-term, but right now, she wanted him beside her.

He nodded and reclined his chair also, in essence making their seats into a bed. He immediately tucked her into his side, allowing her legs to tangle with his. His arm rested across her stomach, mouth just above her ear where he could kiss her hair, and Jenna felt him smile. "Does this mean I'm the Rick O'Connell to your Evie, little librarian?"

Jenna couldn't keep the smile off her face at the mention of her favorite movie. "Let's see. A brash, shoots-first-and-asks-questions-later,   protects-her-at-all-costs-even-against-herself hero? Seems about right."

"Do I need to build you a library for you to knock over?"

Her heart skipped a beat, and her stomach curled with both nerves and desire. "If I had a real library, I definitely wouldn't want to knock it down."

Mark rubbed his thumb back and forth along her hip, and as the plane began to rumble down the runway, the lights dimmed, and she relaxed into him. "I want you to try to sleep," he said gently. "But I also want to know what your perfect library looks like."

"Oh God." She turned on her side, facing him, and closed her eyes. There was a temptation to just say she wanted a library like the one from *Beauty and the Beast*, and that was partially true, but she was never going to live in a castle, so it wasn't exactly practical. "I want it to be at least two stories, with all built-in shelves. Dark wood. I need a spiral staircase to go along with the regular staircase and those sliding ladders that roll along the shelves. A fireplace, big comfy chairs with a lot of pillows, and…" She hesitated, knowing the last bit was probably going to make him sad. It made her sad too. "And windows so I can see outside even if I can't go outside."

Mark's hands tightened on her body, an acknowledgment of her statement without telling her it would be okay or that eventually she would be able to go outside.

Neither of them knew that for sure. In the same way Mark's body was slowly betraying him, Jenna's mind was already betraying her. This wasn't something simple exposure therapy would help. Clearly, if she could only be outside for a minute before she vomited up her guts.

"That sounds beautiful," he said quietly.

Just being near him was helping her relax, and the overload of what happened had made her tired enough that she was starting to get drowsy, but she still wanted to hear him. "Do you have a dream…something? Office?"

"Well," he said. "I've had to think a lot about what I'm going to do once I can't work for Ian anymore. I'm already doing some architectural work for Linear Tactical and I enjoy it, so maybe I'll lean in that direction."

"That sounds amazing."

"If I did, I would need an office and a drafting space. And I'd like it to be warm tones. Maybe dark woods like your library or a cherry. Bright lights to make sure I can see, and some nice windows for the natural light." He moved one of his hands up to stroke her hair slowly.

"Tell me more." It came out half yawn, half demand.

"It could be nice to have a doorway into another office where there was a whole wall of monitors. More monitors than most people would ever use at one time. But I think I know someone who might like that. With a comfortable couch to take breaks and a coffeemaker, so no one has to go down to the kitchen."

Even with her eyes closing, Jenna's lips curled into a smile. "See? Designing a house already."

"Who knows? Maybe I could be good at it."

She was fading now, her body craving the safety of sleep, and she focused on the movement of Mark's hand in her hair. Somewhere far away, she thought she heard him say something else, but she was already gone.

When Jenna woke, Mark wasn't next to her anymore. Her heart deflated a little before she heard the low voices nearby. Both Ian and Mark.

"Do we need to go somewhere more private?" Ian asked him.

"No," Mark said. "Jenna already knows, if she wakes up. And it's not like my peripheral neuropathy is going to be a secret forever."

"It could be." Ian's voice was serious. "There're any number of reasons you could use to say you didn't want to be in the field anymore. No one has to know your business but you, Mark."

There was a pause, and Jenna curled closer under a blanket that hadn't been there when she fell asleep.

"I don't want to hide it. Hiding it makes me want to feel ashamed of it, and I don't. Is it hard? Hell yes. I don't love the feeling of being out of control of my own body. But this is what's happening to me. I can't run from it, and I can't ignore it. If I do, someone's going to get hurt."

"Well," Ian said, "I respect you for that decision. And no one is going to give you shit about it on my watch, I promise you that."

"I appreciate that."

"So, is this *the* conversation?" Ian asked.

Mark sighed. "I guess so. We both knew it was coming. I love what we do, and the idea of hanging that up is terrifying. But what happened two days ago back at the hospital? I can't help but think it's partially on me."

Ian huffed a laugh. "Do I really have to tell you that you're not responsible for the actions of a terrorist?"

"I know that. But I am responsible for letting the man who tried to kill our victim get away. My leg went dead, Ian. I let someone run straight back to Joaquin and tell him the robot was alive and protected. She could have died because of me."

"I've seen the footage. Nobody else even figured out the guy wasn't a real doctor. You saved her life way before your leg gave you shit."

"Maybe. But what about Jenna? Obviously, Joaquin knows how involved she is if he sent all those robots after her last night. That robot at the hospital could've told him she was there."

"Joaquin isn't a fool. He's probably known about Jenna all along. There's no point in carrying guilt that isn't yours, Outlaw."

Jenna would've high-fived Ian if she'd been at the table. Mark wasn't responsible for any of these attacks.

"I know." Mark took a breath, and Jenna could have sworn it was shaky. "How did you do it?"

"Do what?"

Mark laughed, but it didn't sound like humor. "Keep your shit together when Wavy was taken? When she could have died?"

"I absolutely did not keep my shit together," Ian said. "I don't know. Maybe it looked like I did, but I was falling apart. Like the thing that was keeping me tied to the earth was crumbling, and I couldn't do anything about it. Hell, it's still hard for me to let her out of my sight." He laughed.

"Which is why it nearly gives me a heart attack every time she tries to ditch her security detail."

"Understandable." There was a hesitant silence before Mark sighed again. "I guess this will be my last official Zodiac assignment, then. I can't guarantee to keep people safe, and questioning myself on missions is going to keep them even less safe."

"I'm sorry to see you go," Ian said. "But just because you're not directly working for me anymore doesn't mean you're not part of the Zodiac family. Whatever you decide to do, whatever you need, I'll help you."

"Thank you. When I have a clue what I'm doing, I'll let you know."

Ian chuckled again. "I think you know exactly what you're doing. And I think you're going to be in Oak Creek a lot more now, aren't you? Maybe permanently?"

"I don't know what you're talking about," he said, but they both laughed.

Jenna heard the shifting of seats and didn't bother to close her eyes as Mark appeared beside her.

"I didn't know you were awake," he said quietly, lying beside her again and resuming the position she'd fallen asleep in. "Was hoping I could sneak away and be back before you knew I was gone."

"Sorry."

"How much did you hear?"

She winced. "Most of it. Hope that's okay."

Leaning in, Mark kissed her forehead. "It's not anything you don't already know. I wanted to talk to Ian while it was just the two of us. And I don't want to have secrets from you anyway."

Her face flushed pink. "The way you say things, it's like you've already decided something."

She was careful to talk around it. She knew enough to

know her heart was fragile, and as much as the idea of permanence terrified her, it was also what she wanted more than anything.

Mark had hit the nail a little too closely when he'd called her out about lying to her friends. She was embarrassed and lonely, and the idea of having someone who knew everything was intoxicating.

But how could it ever be real?

"How much do you want me to tell you?" he asked. "Because if you heard what I said to Ian, then you know that I have changes coming in my life. And yes, I've been thinking a lot about them and who might be involved in them."

Instinctually, Jenna curled up more. She shook her head. "I know we're the same in some ways," she said. "I know we understand each other. But I need to ask why you would want to be with someone like me? I don't know if you want a family, but how would that work? What kind of mother can't go to her children's sports games because she can't be outside? What kind of person lets a past enemy control her entire life? I get tired of me, and there's no way for me to leave myself behind."

Mark studied her, and the look in his eyes made her heart pound. She saw complete understanding and trust there. Maybe more than that. "Do you like me, Jenna?"

It wasn't the question she was expecting. "Yes."

"Do you like being around me?"

She nodded. He made her feel safe when no one else managed to.

"Are you okay if we keep doing what we've been doing?"

Jenna laughed. "Yes."

The idea of suddenly not touching him was unthinkable. Now that she'd had him, and felt both the tenderness and the strength he held, she very well could get addicted.

"Then, for now," Mark whispered, "that's all it has to be.

Until this is over and neither of us has a million things on our mind or is worrying about taking down a terrorist. Then, after, we can talk about all the stuff we haven't had a chance to. Sound good?"

"Sounds good." She breathed out a breath in relief.

Mark was right. They had things to do that were more important right now than the future. The future could wait for a few days.

"Think you could get some more rest?" he asked.

"Maybe. But you can't sneak away again."

He smiled, and her heart flipped at the sight of it. "Wouldn't dream of it, sweetheart."

Jenna closed her eyes and faded once again into his warmth.

Chapter 20

By the time they reached the hospital in San Diego, Emily Richardson, who'd been arrested in the middle of robbing a clothing store, was not only still alive, she was awake and talking.

Law enforcement was at a loss for what to do with her. She'd been in the middle of breaking the law when she'd been arrested, but all the officers' reports had said the same thing: she'd been nearly lifeless when they'd interacted with her. Cold, shut down… a *robot*.

Like the other robots, her system had started failing after her arrest. Except this time, the hospital staff had been able to get the medicines she needed into her system much sooner since Jenna already knew in which way to direct them.

The most important thing was that Emily's memories were mostly intact. The tail in her system hadn't had enough time to do its job correctly before the other meds began fighting it.

Finally the break they'd been hoping for.

The young woman in the hospital bed was pale, confused, and scared, but medically thriving. The memory compound was working more each minute. Local law enforcement didn't like that federal agents had taken over the case, but Jenna, Mark, and Ian had the freedom they needed to get information.

Mark and Ian had both gone in to question Emily, but she'd refused to talk to them, immediately panicked. They hadn't pushed—neither of them wanting to traumatize the woman or cause any sort of regression.

So now it was Jenna's turn to try.

Mark and Ian were watching from the security cameras set up in the room, and Mark had given Jenna an earpiece so they could offer suggestions or questions Jenna may not think of.

"Hi, Emily." Jenna walked into the hospital room and closed the door behind her. "My name is Jenna. I need to ask you a few questions if that's okay. No need to be nervous."

Emily immediately stiffened. "Are you a nurse or a cop?"

Jenna smiled. "Neither, actually, but I am here to help you, and I can promise you that nothing you say to me will get you in any sort of trouble."

"Really?"

"Yes. The only thing my colleagues and I are interested in is helping catch the people who did this to you and stop them from doing it to anyone else."

The other woman still looked pretty nervous. "Okay."

"Tell me anything you remember about what happened to you."

Emily's eyes immediately filled with tears, and Jenna took her hand. She knew what it was like to be in a hospital and not sure who to trust or what to say. Grabbing a chair with her free hand, Jenna pulled it up next to the bed.

"I'm sorry," the girl said. "It's a little overwhelming. I feel better than I did a few hours ago, but my brain still feels cloudy."

"You were drugged, so that's completely understand-able." Jenna used the most soothing tone she could.

"Jenna." Mark's deep voice came on through the transmitter in her ear. "Try to help her focus on small bits at a time. That should be less overwhelming for her."

"How about we discuss specifics?" Jenna said. "What's your job?"

Emily immediately looked calmer. This was a question she could handle. "I work as an IT manager at a bank."

Another robot with some sort of expertise in computers. Jenna wasn't surprised at all.

"Where?"

"Seattle."

Not the first robot who was far away from home when they were released.

"Okay," Jenna said, squeezing the girl's hand. "Do you know where you are now?"

She wiped tears off her cheeks and sniffled. "Uh, yeah. They told me I was in San Diego. My boyfriend is coming."

Jenna smiled. "That's good. I know you will appreciate having a familiar face here with you. Do you remember anything about how you got here?"

Emily took a deep breath, steadier. "Yeah. I mean, not everything, but a little. The last thing I remember was that I was leaving work and it was late. I was going to my car, and I know there was someone behind me."

"When was that, do you know?"

"Monday night. What day is it now?"

"It's Thursday," Jenna told her gently. The woman had lost days of her life.

Emily squeezed her hand tightly, and Jenna gripped it back. "The rest I remember is like a dream. I walked into this clothing store, and I had a gun. I have no idea why I had a gun. I've never touched a gun in my life. But I couldn't do anything but point it at people. It's like I wasn't in control of myself at all."

Jenna nodded. "I believe you. That's the drugs we were talking about. They affected your choices."

"I forced everybody to leave the store. Why would I do that? I have no idea. Then the cops came, and there was this...*pain*. It was the worst I'd ever felt in my life."

That was the tail Joaquin's scientists had put in the subjectification compound. As soon as Emily had done what she was supposed to do, it started to hurt.

"You're not in pain now, right?"

"No, it hasn't hurt that way since I woke up in the hospital." Emily shifted in the bed. "Did I steal something? Or shoot someone? Is that what I did?"

Jenna shook her head. "No, neither of those things, I promise."

"That's good, I guess."

"Is there anything about the store that you can remember? Anything you did after you made everyone leave?"

Jenna didn't want to mention computers or lead Emily in that direction. She needed the woman to remember on her own.

Emily rubbed her forehead. "I had to do something. I don't know how to explain it."

"I understand. You were compelled." That was the chemical subjectification in a nutshell.

"That sounds ridiculous when you say it out loud. Like I was hypnotized or something."

"It's the *or something*," Jenna explained gently. "And it's real. Anything you can remember will help us. It doesn't matter how small or strange it might seem to you."

"Fine. It's hazy, but what I remember from the store after I kicked everyone out was...working on a computer."

Bingo.

"Tell me about that." Jenna kept her voice neutral.

"Really? Don't you think that's just my brain mixing up my job with what happened? Why would I break in to a clothing store, kick everyone out at gunpoint, then send some sort of transmission via the dark web?"

"Wait. What?" Jenna had been expecting Emily to mention a server—maybe to even remember hacking it. But *sending* a transmission?

Especially via the dark web.

Movies liked to make out the darknet as some sort of evil catchall, consisting of black markets, encryption, and political dissidents.

All of that was true.

But it wasn't all criminal activity. The darknet was basically a subset of the deep web, which was all content on the internet not indexed by search engines.

And yes, there were very definitely forums and chat boards. If someone wanted to send messages that couldn't be traced, the dark web was the place to do it.

"I told you it sounded crazy," Emily whispered.

"No, it doesn't," Jenna corrected.

But it did change everything about how she'd been looking at these government servers. Joaquin hadn't been gathering information; he'd been *sending* it.

"Is she legit?" Mark asked in her ear. Jenna didn't respond verbally, but she nodded so they were sure to see her.

"You accessed Tor via the store's computer?" Jenna asked Emily.

Her eyes got a little bigger. "You know stuff about the darknet?"

Tor—The Onion Router—was an open-source web browser that kept its users anonymous and was the only way to access the darknet. Jenna used it regularly and knew more about the dark web than Emily probably ever would.

"Yeah, a little. Keep going."

Emily hunched down a little. "It just gets weirder from there. Rather than going straight onto Tor, I was...*compelled*, like you said, to hack into a nearby hidden server and send the messages through that. I know that doesn't make any sense."

It made more sense than she knew. "Do you remember anything about the message itself?"

"Not most of it. All I remember is some sort of count-down. Sixty-eight hours."

Just short of three days. Whatever Joaquin was planning was happening then.

"I need to get back to my own computer to figure out what this all means." Jenna was saying it to Mark and Ian more than Emily.

"Do you really think it means something?" Emily asked.

"Definitely."

Mark's voice came into Jenna's ear. "I know you want to go, but see if she remembers anything before the clothing store. She was held for over two days."

He was right, and while Emily was comfortable talking to Jenna, she should take advantage of it with more questions, no matter how much she wanted to get back to her worksta-tion and see if she could make more sense of the situation with this new intel.

"Can you tell me anything more about what happened before you got to the clothing store?"

"Yeah, but that's weird too."

Jenna smiled at her. "Weird doesn't necessarily mean incorrect."

"After I was taken, I woke up in a room that... Well, it looked kind of like a dentist's office. I was in the chair, and I couldn't move." Emily's voice dropped to a whisper, and Jenna reached over and squeezed her hand. "I had an IV in, but I could see they had drawn blood. The vials were on the counter next to me."

"I'm sure that was scary."

"There were three or four doctors, and they were all arguing. But I was scared and they'd drugged me, so I didn't understand what they were talking about." She dropped her head. "I was crying. Begging them to let me go."

How many times had Jenna begged to be let go when she'd been taken? Most people liked to think they would be strong—would never beg their captors for anything. Would keep their pride and dignity, no matter what.

Only someone who'd lived through the hell of real captivity understood that pride and dignity were often the first to fall.

"I would've begged too," Jenna told her. "I would've promised anything to get myself out. That's nothing to be ashamed of."

"They didn't let me go. They just kept arguing with each other."

"Do you remember anything at all they were arguing about?"

"No. It was stuff I didn't understand. Something about the deadline for the sale and me being crispy and ink on my fingers." She shook her head. "But I didn't have any ink on my fingers. I checked."

They were losing her—now she really was starting not to make sense. But it was understandable. She'd already been through so much. "Emily, I think it's probably best for you to get some sleep. I know everything is confused in your head, but you've done an amazing job explaining it all as best you can."

"Jenna," Mark said, "show her the picture of Joaquin. See if she recognizes him."

Jenna took out her phone and flipped it around to show the picture of Joaquin taken by a Zodiac agent last year at someone's wedding. "We'll try to get a sketch artist here to see if you can remember the features of any of the doctors. But do you happen to recognize this man?"

As soon as Emily saw the picture of Joaquin, she wrapped her arms around her head and began sobbing. Jenna jumped up, nearly knocking her chair over. She hadn't been prepared for that reaction.

Had Joaquin put some other blocker into the compound that would cause a reaction in any robot who tried to talk about him?

She put her phone away and reached out to try to soothe Emily. "Shh. It's gone. His picture is gone. I'm sorry. Is your head hurting again? Are you in pain?"

Emily was crying loudly enough that two nurses came running in.

"I'm sorry, you'll have to leave," one of them said.

Ignoring them, Jenna squeezed Emily's hand. "Does it hurt? Tell me where it hurts, Emily."

She shook her head. "It doesn't hurt. But that man…"

One of the nurses was pulling on Jenna's arm, while the other was looking at Emily's vitals and chart.

Jenna let herself be pulled slowly. She didn't know if she'd get another chance to talk to Emily like this. "What about him? What about that man?"

Emily lowered her arms, but she was still crying. "He killed one of the doctors right in front of me. Shot him. Said if the doctors couldn't do their job by the deadline, he'd find someone who could."

Chapter 21

"Where the hell is Callum?" Mark asked Ian from the conference room where they'd been watching Jenna's conversation with Emily. "That woman just admitted that she witnessed Joaquin murder someone in front of her. Let's quit fucking around and arrest him."

"I don't know where he is. He should've already been here."

"We need to let him know what Emily said."

Ian leaned back in his chair and scrubbed a hand down his face. "Problem is, I'm not sure what she said is enough to get a warrant. Lawyers might argue that a woman who's been arrested is conveniently trying to frame someone else to get herself out of trouble. Not to mention she's talking crazy...crispy ink fingers."

As much as Mark didn't want to admit it, Ian was right. "Yeah, I guess the huge cocktail of drugs in her system doesn't help establish her as a credible witness either."

"Did you understand any of that darknet stuff?"

Mark shrugged. "I know it's real, but that's about it. Computers definitely aren't my area of expertise. Jenna will be able to tell us more, but it sounds like we were barking up the wrong tree, thinking Joaquin was trying to siphon info from the servers."

"Honestly, the dark web stuff makes more sense to me."

"How so?"

Ian crossed his arms over his chest. "If Joaquin was trying to get to the info held on the government servers… why use the robots and send them to locations all over the country?"

Mark nodded. "Agreed. Why not just hack them? Would be easier and more efficient."

"Exactly. But if I'm not mistaken, the dark web doesn't have to be accessed from a special location."

"You're right." Jenna walked through the door, frown creasing her brow. "Joaquin could access the dark web anywhere."

Mark got up and handed her a bottle of water. She chugged it all down at once. "So, what's his endgame?"

"I don't know. I just know what we thought we knew was wrong." She tossed the bottle in the recycling bin. "I need to rewatch the footage of Emily and me. There's more. I'm missing it, but I know there's more. I'm making too many mistakes."

Mark hated the way stress blanketed her features. He grabbed her and pulled her into his chest. "Hey, librarian, you're not making mistakes. You're taking each step based on the intel you have. As the intel changes, our steps change. You're not doing anything wrong."

"I'll avoid turning this into some awkward group hug situation, but I concur with Outlaw, Jenna," Ian said. "Don't doubt yourself. We're not doubting you."

She seemed a little stronger as she pulled away, and that was all Mark could ask for right now. "I'm not sure where to focus my attention, to be honest."

"On the sixty-eight-hour countdown." He and Ian said it at the same time.

Mark nodded. "We now have confirmation of some sort of attack or something in just under sixty-eight hours."

Jenna sat down at the laptop she'd brought into the hospital. "Emily was in that clothing store seven hours ago, so I'm going to start a timer for sixty hours to be conservative."

She clicked on the keyboard, and a few moments later, a countdown timer started on her screen. "We have exactly two and a half days to figure out what Joaquin is doing and stop him."

A phone rang in Ian's hand. "It's Callum."

"About damned time," Mark muttered. They needed him here so they could come up with a game plan.

"You're on speaker again, Callum. Are you en route?"

"No, I'm not coming. I'm staying undercover. I only have a few minutes to talk."

Jenna's eyes got big. "I thought helping get us out of the attack on the lab compromised your position in Joaquin's organization."

"They suspect me but can't prove it, so I'm safe for the time being."

Ian shook his head. "Callum, are you sure about this? The last undercover agent they found—"

"Trust me, I remember the pieces. But there's something going on. *Big.* I don't know what, and I'm not exactly sure when, but I've got to keep digging."

"We know the when," Jenna said. "Exactly two and a half days from now. The latest robot, Emily, provided that intel."

"Okay. That gives me something to work with."

"Emily also witnessed Joaquin killing one of his own

team," Mark put in. "Although we don't think she would be the most credible witness in court."

There was a slight pause before Callum spoke. "I haven't been able to get close to Joaquin himself. He's too smart for that. But I'll keep pressing and try to figure out what's going down in two and a half days. I've got to go."

"We'll do the same," Ian said. "Be careful, brother. I like you better whole than in pieces."

"Trust me, so do I." The call clicked off.

Jenna was firing on all cylinders at the workstation on the bus. She used damned near superhero-level powers. She had four monitors running different…stuff. Hell if Mark knew what most of it was.

"The key here is the dark web. Like you guys said, there was no reason for Joaquin to piggyback off government servers if he was trying to send messages. He could access The Onion Router wherever he wanted." She never looked away from the screens or stopped typing as she spoke.

"Onion Router is really the name for how you access the dark web?"

"Don't look at me. I didn't come up with the name. It was something to do with peeling back layers. Everyone calls it Tor."

Mark shook his head. "And anyone can access the dark web?"

"If they're determined to, they can. Pretty easily, actually. But it's not like the regular web where you can just Google stuff once you're there. If you don't know where you're going, you'll basically be sitting around doing nothing."

"But Joaquin didn't need the government servers to access what he needed on the dark web."

She stopped typing. "Definitely not. My thinking is that he's piggybacking off the government servers to add some credibility to whatever messages he's sending out."

Mark crossed his arms over his chest. "Like: *I'm about to do this big, bad thing, and you can believe me because, look, I already have access to the US government's secrets*."

"Yes, exactly like that."

That made a twisted sort of sense.

"But—" Jenna turned and waggled her eyebrows at him "—I'm going to use Joaquin's arrogance against him."

"How so?"

"I wrote an algorithm that is checking the darknet for messages or data that was sent when each robot broke in to their building. I don't know what data it will give us, but it will give us something."

Mark waggled his own eyebrows. "You're super sexy when you're brilliant, you know that?"

She blew him a kiss then turned back to the screens. On the top right corner of them all was the countdown. Fifty-five hours left now.

Mark got up and poured them both cups of coffee. He had a feeling that was going to be a staple for the next two days.

Something had been bugging him all afternoon. "It's still weird, right? That Joaquin would send the robots like that if he didn't have to. Everything we know about him suggests he's strategic—sending robots where they can get caught and giving us potential clues…doesn't seem smart."

Jenna shifted a little in her chair but didn't turn from her screens. "Maybe his ego got the best of him. He wanted to show what his robots could do."

"Or *test* what they could do."

Now she turned around. "That would make sense. Maybe the ones that have been caught are only the tips of the iceberg. Maybe some weren't even break-ins. Maybe…"

She turned back around, muttering to herself, typing frantically. Mark just let her work.

"Tests," she said a few minutes later. "Of course. You're the brilliant one now, Outlaw. I can't believe this didn't occur to me before. I need to add all the servers. It'll take longer, but it's going to give us actionable intel."

He'd thought she'd been working fast before, but now it was really impressive. A few minutes later, the security monitor near the front of the bus beeped and clicked on. Mark got up to check out who was approaching. When he saw it was Ian, he opened the door.

"How's it going?" Ian asked.

"Evidently, I'm brilliant and we're in the process of making some sort of big breakthrough. Pay no attention to the part of the bus that's on fire because Jenna's fingers are moving so fast."

Ian chuckled. "All that seems about par for the course."

"I just make sure she has food and coffee and basically stay out of her way."

Ian's smile got bigger. "That's what all of us do with Jenna."

It was a little over an hour later when Jenna scooted back from her workstation and stood. "Holy shit."

"What?" Mark and Ian both said at the same time.

"Vegas."

"What about it?" Mark asked.

She poured herself a cup of coffee. "I wrote a program that collected any messages that pinged off any of the secret government servers over the past two weeks."

"You can do that?" Ian asked.

She half hid her face behind the coffee cup. "Um…legally?"

Ian held out a hand. "Don't even tell me. Just tell us what you found."

"Whatever is happening in—" she turned back to look at the screens to get the countdown "—fifty-three hours and thirty-seven minutes is happening in Vegas. I couldn't pinpoint more than that."

Mark grabbed his phone and started looking up events. "Looks like there's a couple big concerts and some sort of Broadcasters of America convention—all will have twenty thousand plus people in attendance. There's an NBA game too."

Ian rubbed his eyes. "Those could all be big terrorist attack locations. I need to get law enforcement on this, stat."

Jenna nodded. "I'm sorry there isn't more info to provide."

Mark reached over and squeezed her shoulder. "A time and place? That's pretty damned important intel."

"He's right, Jenna." Ian already had his phone out. "It gives us more to work with than you think."

"I should hopefully be able to get a list of robots who successfully completed their missions and weren't caught, based on what government servers were used. I'll run those dates and times against local cameras and see what we can find."

Ian nodded. "Everything helps."

"I have no idea what state they'll be in. Joaquin's scientists could've programmed them to go into some sort of sleeper mode, or, honestly, they could be dead. But that would seem like a waste. There are at least another dozen robots we weren't aware of."

"Okay, keep on it," Ian said. "Report your findings directly to Omega Sector so they can move on them. I'll be working with them to try to figure out what's going to happen in Vegas."

"Is it okay if we head home and do this?" Mark asked. "We love your bus, but I think Jenna would like to sleep in her own bed."

And he planned to be sleeping there with her, but that didn't need to be said.

But more importantly, her house was where she felt most safe.

"Absolutely. You've done your part, Jenna. We never would've made this progress if it weren't for you. Everything else, you should be able to do from home. I'll see when the plane can be ready, and you guys keep the bus with you in case we need to move quickly again."

She slid over to Mark and eased against him. He wrapped an arm around her, pulling her close.

"That would be great. This has taken a lot out of me. If I get any further info, I'll definitely make sure to pass it along. But yeah, I feel like things are out of my hands now."

"You did a good job. We'll handle it from here." Ian nodded at them both then headed off the bus.

Jenna turned to Mark. "I really am ready to go home." She smiled. "The robots' situation may be out of my hands, but I'll bet I can find something else to keep my hands full."

He kissed her and began backing her toward the bedroom. "I'm more than happy to help with that."

Chapter 22

Jenna stared at the screens facing her. She felt like she was seeing code swim in front of her eyes, which happened sometimes when she slipped into a flow state and nothing else mattered besides the data that was before her.

The program she'd written—sloppy, ugly, but got the job done—had provided them with the names and locations of sixteen other robots. She'd sent the info to Ian, and the team was carefully picking them up.

They'd all be administered the recovery drug compound. Because they were early versions of the robots, it should work just as well as it did on Emily. From there, it would be a matter of working with them as they recovered their memories and seeing if that brought them any more clues about Joaquin's upcoming event.

The countdown was less than forty-eight hours now.

In just a couple hours, as soon as the plane was ready, she and Mark would be back on their way to Oak Creek. Jenna would continue to do whatever was in her power to discover what Joaquin was attempting to pull off in the next two days and stop him.

She'd just be doing it from the comfort and safety of her own home, and she couldn't wait. She and Mark were both pretty damned exhausted.

Case in point, Mark was currently sitting at the table, leaning against the wall of the bus, with his eyes closed, legs up on the seat. The way his chest moved up and down, she knew he was sleeping. But she also knew enough about him that he wasn't sleeping deeply.

The pose was one she recognized: soldier's sleep. He would wake at a moment's notice if she needed him, and the thought made warmth spread through her chest.

Although, she was pretty sure he would wake for her even if he hadn't put himself into a lighter mode of sleeping. He was there when she needed him.

It was addictive. *Outlaw himself* was addictive. Watching him now, she felt her fingers itch to trace the outline of his face. He was obviously still a warrior even in sleep—features rugged and hard.

But he was *her* warrior.

She must've stared too hard because his green eyes blinked open.

"Hey." He smiled slowly, and her breath caught at the beauty of it.

This man didn't just give her butterflies; he gave her a whole damn zoo. "Hey yourself."

He kicked his legs down. "Almost time to head for the airport. Want to get some coffee and some to-go food for on the way?"

"Hell yes," she said. "Although I don't really want fast food. Do you think there's anything else open at this hour?"

He grabbed the keys. "Actually, there's a little twenty-four-hour café. We stopped there on the way to the hospital yesterday. You were still sleeping."

"Oh, perfect."

She settled into her chair and watched him drive. The darkness outside the windows was peaceful, and she knew it was balmy because of the weather report. She wished she could tell Mark to take a detour and head to the beach. One of the things she missed the most about the outside world was the beach.

Jenna fought off the deep feeling of sadness that weighed her down as she wondered if she'd ever be able to be on the beach again.

But that was something she could deal with later, after she was home and had had a full night's sleep in her own bed. After they had stopped whatever Joaquin was planning.

Before long, Mark was pulling into the parking lot of a small coffee shop, the lights bright in the early morning. He parked and looked at her, and she could tell he was just as tired as she was. "What do you want?"

"To drink, I'll take something with chai," she said, not wanting the harsh, pure abrasiveness of coffee at the moment. "Food...I'm not sure. What do they serve?"

"Apparently they're known for their chicken fingers. I know that sounds nuts, but that's what everyone was talking about in line. Some sort of crispy breading. I think I'm going to try them."

"Yeah, me too."

"You got it." He took a moment and put his hands on both armrests, leaning over her and kissing her gently. "I'll be right back."

The door opened and closed, and she let her head fall back against the chair and stared at the ceiling. After so many days feeling like she was constantly in a state of movement and urgency, it felt weird to be standing still. Like the odd sensation when you'd been on a boat too long and suddenly came back to dry land. It took a while to get used to stillness.

So for right now, she'd just be happy about her upcoming chicken fingers. Not just chicken fingers, *crispy* chicken fingers.

Crispy fingers.

Jenna's smile faded as Emily's words from yesterday came back to her. God, how had she not realized before what the woman was talking about.

Jenna rushed over to her computer system and brought up the recording of the interview. It didn't take long to find the section she was looking for.

"Do you remember anything at all they were arguing about?"

"No. It was stuff I didn't understand. Something about the deadline for the sale and me being crispy and ink on my fingers. But I didn't have any ink on my fingers. I checked."

Not *ink* fingers…*zinc* fingers. As in, zinc finger nucleases. ZFNs were a type of DNA-binding proteins.

And Jenna was willing to bet the scientists talking around Emily had said CRISPR, not *crispy*. CRISPR/Cas9…the most important technology in the world when it came to gene editing—a way of finding a specific piece of DNA inside a cell.

Those two factors were the very basics of the subjectification research Jenna had developed while she was in captivity. Emily would have no frame of reference for those terms, so her brain had turned them into something else.

Jenna watched the footage again, this time paying more attention to the rest of their conversation and when Emily freaked out over seeing Joaquin. Except this time, Jenna didn't focus on the fact that Joaquin had shot someone in from of Emily.

She focused on the *why*.

If the doctors couldn't do their job by the deadline, Joaquin would find someone who could.

Deadlines.

Scientists.

Countdowns.

Sale.

It all came together for Jenna in a moment, and once the pieces fell into place, it all made perfect sense.

Joaquin was planning to sell the subjectification technology. That was what the countdown was to. That was why he'd had the robots ping off government servers—to get the word out about what he had for sale and to demonstrate what it could do at the same time.

But evidently, he'd run into some sort of problem if he was killing scientists just a day ago. He didn't have the capacity to make the compound universal yet.

Jenna grinned. There weren't many people in the world who had the expertise to do that. She was one of them, but she sure as hell wouldn't be helping him.

She needed to get this info to Ian. They didn't need to waste their time narrowing down potential terrorist attack locations in Vegas. They all needed to figure out the meeting place.

Jenna's head began buzzing with potential ways to find it. She needed to get Kendrick Foster and his wife Neo on this too. It was going to take all of them working around the clock to get the intel they needed before the deadline.

She didn't want to get up when she heard the tap on the door a few minutes later, but she knew she had to. She checked the exterior cameras and saw Mark scanning the parking lot with a cup carrier in one hand and a bag of food in the other, and she pressed the open button.

"Here you go," Mark said, handing her the cup carrier.

He stumbled and fell, the cups falling onto the stairs between them, spilling.

"Mark!" Oh God, was it his legs again? He was halfway in the bus and halfway on the ground, and even though her skin was crawling being so close to the door, she crouched next to him—

There was a dart in his neck.

Terror tore through her. "Mark!"

She shoved her hands under his arms, trying to pull him inside, but he was dead weight. Completely unconscious.

She knew this meant they were being attacked, but no way in hell was she shoving him out of the bus to save herself.

"Come on." She strained. She was strong, but he had nearly a hundred pounds on her. That and the awkward angle of trying to pull him up the bus stairs made getting him inside impossible.

She'd have to go outside if she wanted to save him.

Adrenaline slammed through her veins, but she refused to let panic take over. Hunching her shoulders and taking a deep breath, she leaped over Mark, not focusing on anything but pushing him inside.

Up, up, up. Come on.

She wasn't sure if the heavy footsteps she heard were real or only in her head, but either way, she was out of time.

"Please." She didn't know who she was begging—Mark, her muscles, or the enemy closing in. "*Please.*"

She got him up another stair. She was almost there. Just a couple more inches—

She felt a pinch in her neck, and a few seconds later, her hands went slack, Mark slipping from her grasp. She fell hard onto the steps.

As her vision spiraled into darkness, the last thing she saw was three men grabbing Mark and hauling him away—chicken fingers spilling onto the dark asphalt.

Chapter 23

Mark's head pounded with pain, and he swore. What the fuck happened? His legs had been tingling, but he hadn't felt them go out. He'd been holding out the drinks to Jenna, and then…the ground. That was all he remembered.

Right now, it felt like he had the biggest hangover known to man. What the hell? He tried to move but couldn't. This definitely had to be his neuropathy.

Forcing his eyes open, he tried to move again, and realized it wasn't his neuropathy at all. He was in a room he didn't recognize, in a chair like the one Emily had described. It wasn't a dentist's chair, but it seemed like it. His arms and legs were strapped down.

Across from him, Jenna was in a similar chair, also tied down. There was nothing else about the room to tell him where they were.

He closed his eyes again for a brief moment.

When he'd scanned the parking lot, they'd been alone. How the fuck did Joaquin find them? There wasn't a question of who it was. The only person with a motive to take

Jenna was Joaquin—Mark wasn't arrogant enough to think he was the reason they were taken.

Her eyes were closed, and she was still except for the slow, rhythmic motion of one hand. He recognized it for what it was, some sort of stress-release movement.

"Jenna."

His voice was rough, and her eyes flew open. "Mark. Thank God." As she looked at him, a tear leaked out of one eye. "You're okay. I wasn't sure if they'd…"

She trailed off, but he knew what she didn't say. She'd been afraid they'd given him something stronger than a tranquilizer. He wouldn't point out that if they'd killed him, they wouldn't have bothered to bring him here.

"My head hurts like a bitch," he said. "What happened?"

Mark scanned the room again, assessing it differently now that he was alert. There was only one interior entrance that he could see, unless there was a door behind him. But based on the countertops and equipment he saw when he turned his head, he didn't think it was likely. A big, rolling bay door was beside them. He couldn't hear anything that indicated if it led outside or to some kind of warehouse.

"They came out of nowhere," she said. "I couldn't get you into the bus. I'm sorry."

He wished he could touch her. "You should've pushed me out and closed the doors."

"No, I wouldn't do that."

"Jenna—"

"No!" she yelled. "I wasn't going to let you die. Please don't tell me I should have. If the roles were reversed, you wouldn't have considered it for a second. Neither did I."

That was true, but he'd give damned near anything—even his own life—if she could be safe right now. Not captured and at the hands of a madman. Again.

"Have you seen anyone?"

She shook her head with a shaky breath. "Not yet. Just you."

Mark locked eyes with her. "We're going to be okay. You hear me? We're going to get out of this."

"Mark, I figured out what's going on right before we were taken. The countdown isn't for a terrorist attack, it's for—"

"Good to see you're awake." The door swung open, and a large man entered, cutting off Jenna's words. Tall and broad, dark hair perfectly styled. He was wearing a black button-down with the sleeves rolled up and some buttons open, like he was about to go out on a yacht. Or to a party.

Joaquin Martinez, in the flesh.

Mark had seen his picture and committed it to memory. In the corner of his eye, he saw Jenna flex her arms, trying to get them loose, but the straps had barely any give to them.

The terrorist walked toward her, and Mark struggled against the restraints, his nerves tingling everywhere. But just like Jenna's, his had no give to them either.

"It's a pleasure to meet you, Dr. Franklin," Joaquin said. "It is doctor, right? You have a PhD in bioengineering and a master's in computer science. Quite impressive."

Jenna didn't respond.

"I stole most of the data from Adil Garrison's lab just before he went to prison, but unfortunately, you were never mentioned by name. So much brilliance and you weren't given any credit—such a crime. I looked for you, you know. Searched through so many scientists that would've been willing to work for Garrison for the right price."

"I wasn't willing to work for him," she spat out.

Joaquin nodded. "Took me embarrassingly long to figure that out. That Garrison would resort to kidnapping to get what he wanted."

"Yeah, imagine that. Some asshole resorting to kidnap-

JANIE CROUCH

ping to get what he wants." Mark tugged at his bound hands to reiterate his point.

Joaquin gave a grim smile. "Touché. I know you're brilliant, Jenna. World-alteringly brilliant. You have my respect for that."

"If you had any respect for me, you wouldn't have me strapped to a damned chair," she snapped.

Mark could no longer see the man's face, but he heard him chuckle. "In my life, everyone is treated like an enemy until they prove themselves otherwise. I'm hoping you will prove yourself not my enemy, Jenna."

Again, silence filled the room.

"I've had some of the best bioengineers in the field working on what I now know is your research, trying to find the key for what I need," Joaquin continued. "If you're as smart as I think you are, I don't need to tell you what I've been up to—you already know."

Jenna's face steeled. "Nope, sorry. I don't know. I must not be as smart as you think. You should probably just let us go."

He clucked his tongue. "Now, that's not very sportsman-like. I think you know exactly what I'm looking for, don't you?"

Mark watched her glare at the man, but he also watched her weigh the options in front of them. Playing along until they could find out where they were and how to get out was by far their best bet.

"Universal subjectification," she gritted out.

Shock tightened Mark's body. *Universal subjectification* was what Jenna had figured out the countdown was to?

"Exactly," Joaquin said. "I knew you were smart. The people working for me haven't been able to do it. So far, they've only been able to synthesize the compounds for specific genetic profiles—the ones you used in your work.

And unfortunately, we're under a bit of a time crunch, so I'm going to need you to produce the universal formula immediately."

Jenna laughed. "I can't. It's not real. There's no way to do it."

"Are you sure about that?" Joaquin's voice was deadly soft.

"Like you said, I'm the expert."

Jenna swallowed, and Mark realized she was bluffing, which was smart. If she gave Joaquin what he wanted, he would have no reason to keep them around.

"Hmm." The sound was long and drawn-out as Joaquin turned and approached Mark. "You see, you might be the expert, Jenna, but you're not the only one. The scientists I have—who know better than to lie to me by now—have told me it *is* possible. They just can't figure out how do it."

"I disagree."

Joaquin's eyes narrowed. "Disagreement isn't an option."

Jenna held her ground. "Well, I'm also going to have to disagree that disagreement isn't an option."

Joaquin didn't continue the argument. He pulled a hand out of his pocket, and the knife blade flashed before Mark could fully register it, pain blazing through him as fire burst inside his thigh.

"Mark!"

Jenna's scream was all he could hear over his own yell and the pain rocketing through his body. He forced himself to control his breathing and focus. It was just pain. He'd dealt with pain before, and he could take it.

The knife now sticking out of his thigh was large, but sharp. A clean wound that would heal. It was enough to tell him Joaquin didn't want him to die.

At least, not yet.

"While you've been such sleepyheads for the past twelve hours, I've looked into you both," Joaquin said casually.

They had been unconscious that long? *Fuck.*

Ian and Callum knew they were missing by now. That was a good thing. But there was no way to tell where they were. In twelve hours, they could be nearly anywhere.

Jenna ignored Joaquin. "Mark? Are you okay?"

He nodded. It was all he could do.

"You two have been almost inseparable for the past few days," Joaquin continued over Jenna. "I've even found images of Mr. Outlawson here carrying you places. I personally think that's a little over the top, but what it tells me is that you two are the key to each other."

Jenna was yanking at her straps until Mark was afraid she would cut herself.

"So, every time you refuse to help me, Outlawson will be the one who gets the pain. And believe me, Jenna, I know how to inflict pain. I know how to make it last, and I know to make sure he survives long enough to take more."

"Jenna," Mark forced out. "I'm okay. Don't do it."

In one smooth movement, Joaquin turned and pulled the knife out of his leg, causing a whole new wave of shuddering pain, and Mark grunted as sweat beaded on his forehead.

But he still shook his head at her.

Just because he'd never been tortured as part of his military service didn't mean he didn't know how to outlast a man like Joaquin at least until the countdown had passed. She didn't have to do this.

"You're going to help me," Joaquin said. "End of story."

"No, I'm not," Jenna said, looking straight at Mark. "Enough people have died because of me."

Good girl.

Joaquin chuckled. "I'm not sure which part of that you

thought was a request. You will help me, one way or another. It's up to you what's left of your boyfriend when you do."

"What's your plan, Joaquin?" Mark asked, trying to deflect the man's attention off Jenna. "What's the end goal here? Selling the ability to subjectify to the highest bidder? What a cliché."

Joaquin shrugged. "Clichés exist for a reason. And one of the beautiful things about being richer than nearly everyone in the world—which I will be once this is done—is you don't have to care about clichés."

He turned back to Jenna. "You have twelve hours to make it happen."

"Twelve hours?" She shook her head. "Even if I believed it could be done, which I do not, twelve hours isn't enough time."

"That's all you have," Joaquin said. "I'm receiving final bids in eighteen hours, and I want time to test the merchandise."

"I won't do it."

"Then I hope your boyfriend likes pain. Because I will hurt him, Jenna. I'll do it again and again and again until you help me, simply to hear him stop screaming. And your deadline will still be the same, so every minute you delay, you make your own job—and his life—harder."

"Don't do it, Jenna," Mark said. "I can take it."

Because thank God Joaquin hadn't had time to dig far enough into Jenna to know her true fears. No doubt the man would use them against her in a heartbeat.

Mark would take every bit of pain he had to if it meant Jenna wasn't terrorized and Joaquin didn't get the ability to make robots out of anyone and everyone.

"What happens if it can't be done?" Jenna asked between ragged breaths. "I'm not playing games with you now. What you're asking for is impossible even if I did my quickest and best work."

Joaquin was truly smiling now. "Find a way. While you were asleep, I also had my scientists do a work-up on your genetic profiles so we could create a subjectification compound for both of you."

"What does that mean, asshole?" Mark asked.

Joaquin glanced at him before turning back to Jenna. "It means that if Jenna fails, I'm injecting you with the formula, and I'll order you to slit your own throat while she watches."

He turned and gestured to the door, and men swarmed in, unbuckling Mark and Jenna from the chairs and getting them up, marching Jenna and dragging Mark to an empty lab down the hallway.

Mark was thrown into another chair and strapped down. This time, it wasn't just hands and feet. More straps across his chest and legs, and one across his forehead, holding him in place.

Jenna was thrown against one of the lab tables, and Mark struggled uselessly against the restraints. Joaquin watched him with a smile on his face, the bloody knife twirling over his fingers.

"Time to get to work, Jenna. Every fifteen minutes you don't have progress, Mark here gets more pain."

Mark was about to tell her not to when one of the thugs shoved cloth into his open mouth and sealed it with duct tape before he could spit it out.

Joaquin simply looked between the two of them, twirling the knife once more. "I don't care about most things, as long as I get my way. But, this?" He pointed back and forth between Mark and Jenna, grinning. "This is going to be fun."

Chapter 24

Mark was strapped to the chair. It was all Jenna could see and think about. Blood had soaked through his pants where Joaquin had stabbed him, and she couldn't watch him go through that again.

But she also couldn't just hand over the kind of power Joaquin was asking for. Nor had she told him she would. He was forcing her hand, and she hadn't corrected him.

Twelve hours. What could she do in twelve hours?

What she'd told him was…mostly true. It was possible that a formula for universal subjectification existed. But even if she were motivated to find it, it would take her way more than twelve hours. Between formulation and testing, it would take *weeks*, not hours.

She wasn't surprised Joaquin had jumped the gun and created a date and time for a sale before he had a final product. It hadn't occurred to him that he would fail. She could use his own arrogance against him.

If she could keep it together when Mark was bound and bleeding a few feet away.

She'd never thought this would be true, but she would

rather be dragged outside and left there as torture than see Mark hurt more. Of course, no way in hell was she giving Joaquin that knowledge. All he'd do was hurt *both* of them.

She was willing to bet they were somewhere near Las Vegas. If they'd really been out for twelve hours, Ian and Callum knew they were missing and were already doing everything in their power to find them.

But it wouldn't be enough. There was no way even all the clout behind Zodiac Tactical would help them now.

Joaquin turned to her from the door. "Now that we have an understanding, I'll bring in my team to assist you."

"No."

Joaquin looked at her and raised his eyebrows. "No? Shall I go to work on Mr. Outlawson's other leg? Maybe cut off a finger?"

"I'm not saying I won't do it. I'm saying no to your team. I work best alone. Do you want me to complete the task, or do you want me to spend time explaining myself to people who you've already told me aren't smart enough to do it?"

Internally, she winced. The people who were working for Joaquin might not have any more choice than she did. But regardless of whether or not they'd chosen this, she wasn't about to give this work to anyone else.

And she didn't want them to figure out she was working *against* Joaquin.

Because no matter what, she wasn't creating a universal subjectification compound for him. She would die first.

And as much as the thought shattered her heart, she would let Mark die first too.

Joaquin raised his hands and smirked. "Fair point. But only as long as I see you making progress."

She kept the rest of her thoughts to herself—that he likely wouldn't know progress if it hit him in the face. But she looked at Mark, and he was watching her carefully.

She wished she could reassure him. This time, she wasn't going to be anyone's pawn, and she wasn't going to be anyone's victim.

But she was also planning to keep both herself and Mark alive.

"Well, settle in if you want to," she said as she turned to familiarize herself with the lab around her. "This isn't exactly action-packed stuff. I'll be using the computer most of the time."

Joaquin laughed like this was one big joke, and she went to sit at the computer, ignoring the fact that he was following her to the seat.

She sat, and he braced himself on the table across from her, the bloodied knife still under his fingers. "Look at me."

She didn't want to, but if she was going to play along, she needed to give this man an appearance of what he wanted.

In the corner of her eye, she saw Mark struggling against the restraints, trying whatever he could to loosen them even a fraction. One of Joaquin's men stepped forward and raised his gun like he was about to hit Mark with it, and she yelled. "Hey!"

Joaquin turned, and the guard stepped back. When he looked at her again, his eyes were narrowed and cold. "That computer is a closed system, and the whole system is being monitored. Trying anything through it will come at a price to your friend."

"Fine." She rose from the chair. "But if we're going to have an agreement, we're going to have an agreement. Your goons can't hit him simply because they fucking feel like it."

Joaquin huffed a laugh. "If it makes you feel better. I'll enjoy hurting him more myself anyway. My men won't touch him."

"But, sir, he was trying—"

Joaquin cut the guard off. "Did I speak to you?"

"No, sir."

"Then both of you get out and go do something useful."

Neither of his subordinates looked happy to be verbally smacked, but they obeyed and left without further argument.

Jenna focused on the computer. She could do this… She could fool Joaquin. She just had to figure out how.

Closing her eyes, she took a long breath and thought through the variables. Joaquin said he wanted to be able to test the product, so there was no way for her to simply give him a dummy formula and expect it to fool him. She had no doubt Mark would die if she did that.

But what if…

She had to show Joaquin something, but it didn't have to be *permanent*. Something that would last just long enough to convince him it was real.

She could do that.

But in order to have it work on whatever random person it was given to, she'd almost have to crack the *real* universal subjectification compound.

It was a risky move. Once she did this, she would make herself expendable. If Joaquin found out her compound was only temporary and had her killed, it wouldn't be difficult for another scientist to put the last pieces of the puzzle together.

It was worth the risk.

All the research files were on the computer. Every test his scientists had completed and the results. She skimmed through them, letting her brain process the info without taking time to read in depth.

They were clever. Not completely on the right track, but there were some interesting test results there.

The current formulas they had created worked almost like a key. You programmed it with the genetic information of the victim, so when it was introduced, it would bind to their DNA and hijack it.

The basic formula for subjectification could work on anyone—it was, in essence, fitting the key in the hole. But it didn't stick to the victim unless the key could *turn* —that only currently worked on DNA with specific markers. Turning the key was where Joaquin's scientists had failed.

She would make a formula that would give the impression that the key was in the hole and had turned—but the victim could metabolize the compound and would naturally come out from under its effects after an hour or two.

Jenna was careful to keep her face and body neutral as she sorted through the data in front of her. It was more important than ever that she not give Joaquin any ideas about her plan.

She blew out a breath to help ease her nerves. It was a risk, and a huge one. Even with twelve hours, it would be close.

She also needed to make Joaquin more comfortable. She didn't know how much he'd been observing his own scientists and how much he knew about the process itself. She couldn't take a chance he might recognize the changes and substitutions she was making.

She looked up and met his eyes. "Fine. I'll do it."

She heard Mark struggle against his gag but ignored him. He had to think she was willing to do this too. At least for now.

Joaquin tilted his head to the side as he studied her. "You mean it."

She nodded. "Yes. But not if you're going to hurt Mark every fifteen minutes. I can't work that way. If you want me to hit that deadline, I'm going to need every second. So, change your methods."

Joaquin watched her carefully, studying her like an eagle might look down at a field mouse. "Fine. But if you don't hit the deadline and provide a viable formula for me, he will suffer in ways you can't imagine before he dies."

Jenna had to force herself not to blanch. If she didn't pull this off, Mark would be the one who would ultimately pay for it. "I'll get it done, and you'll have a working compound."

"Clock is ticking."

"I need food. And coffee," she added quickly because she really was going to need that. "Clearly, neither Mark nor I have eaten in over a day, and I won't be able to do twelve hours of work without it."

Joaquin looked like he was going to refuse.

She rolled her eyes. "What could I possibly do to screw you over with food and coffee? It's not like I have someone on the outside to put a file in a cake."

That made him smile. "I'll give you one thing, Jenna," he said. "You're a more entertaining prisoner than I imagined. Be careful, or I'll be tempted to keep you around."

All she did was stare at him until he smiled again. "Fine. You'll have your food and your coffee. I'm sealing you in here, and I'll be back. Keep in mind there are cameras with audio covering every inch of the lab. You're being monitored."

He sauntered out of the hermetic doors, and they sealed with a final-sounding click. Her shoulders dropped, and she leaned on the table for a second.

Mark grunted, and she walked over and pulled the gag out of his mouth.

"Don't do this."

"Stop, Mark." She shook her head, not looking at him. There was no way to tell him the plan without risking it, so she had to keep it away from everyone. Even him. "I'm going to do this, and you're going to be fine."

"Jenna. Please. My life is not worth it. No one life is worth what you'll be giving Joaquin the capacity to do."

She refused to look in his direction, because one look in those green eyes and the carefully constructed facade she was keeping up would break.

She knew how much this would hurt him. To be strapped down and helpless, unable to protect her. But he'd protected her so much in the last days and weeks. It was okay. He'd been there for her through everything, and he'd saved her life in more ways than one.

This time, it was her turn.

Chapter 25

Mark could see Jenna out of the corner of his eye, working over at one of the lab's far tables. Her location choice was to deliberately create distance from him.

The message was clear: she was doing this work for Joaquin, and she wasn't interested in discussing it.

He had so many problems with that. From the knowledge that he must have let his guard down for Joaquin's thugs to have gotten the drop on them so quickly, to the fact that once Jenna completed what Joaquin wanted, they were both dead anyway.

When Joaquin had first left to get the food, Mark had tried arguing with Jenna—again—even though they were being observed. While she'd applied pressure to his wound enough to make sure he wouldn't die of blood loss, he'd leaned in close.

"Don't do this. No matter what. You can't, librarian."

Those brown eyes had met his. "I'm not going to let you die a horrible death if I can prevent it."

"You can't. You know that. I—"

She'd cupped his cheek. "You have to trust me. And if the roles were reversed…"

That was it. She'd moved away from him without another word and gotten to work.

But she was right. If the roles were reversed, would he be able to watch Jenna be tortured when he could prevent it?

No. Mark would let the whole world burn to the ground first.

He leaned his head back against the seat. He was weak, partially from the drugs remaining in his system, and definitely from the stab wound and blood loss. In a way, it was a blessing he was in restraints. He wasn't able to move his leg and make it worse.

But that didn't mean he hadn't been trying every method he could to get out of them.

"Are you okay?" he asked Jenna quietly.

"I'm fine," she said.

The words were short and clipped. She wasn't fine. She was the furthest thing from fine. The only thing that would make this worse was if Joaquin had forced her to do it outside.

Joaquin sauntered in with someone following him and carrying a tray. "Food and coffee, as promised. But nobody is feeding him, Jenna. If you think it's worth the time, you can do it."

He could sense her glaring at Joaquin, though she wasn't in his sight until she stalked over to the tray and grabbed a sandwich and one of the disposable cups of coffee off it.

"You don't have to," he said to her. "I'm fine."

"We're in this together." Her features were pinched. "You need food. You're injured."

"And he's going to be more injured if you take too much time with him."

Jenna ignored Joaquin and tore off a piece of the sandwich and fed it to him, following it up with a sip of coffee. The coffee tasted burned and like the bottom of a day-old pot, but it was good to have any kind of hydration.

A couple more bites and Mark was finished. With the state his body was in, he wasn't going to be able to keep much more down. "No more. Go do what you need to do."

She nodded and disappeared out of his line of sight once more with her food. He wished he were turned just a fraction so he could see her. Just so he could see her. If this was going to be the last day of his life—and he wasn't accepting that yet—he wanted to be able to see the woman he loved.

And he did love her. It was beyond falling now. Jenna was…

She was *everything*. And right now, he needed to give her whatever she needed to make it through this. Because he'd gotten so caught up in the *roles reversed* statement that he hadn't focused on the most important thing—she'd told him to trust her.

He knew Jenna well enough to know she wasn't simply going to hand Joaquin the key to taking over the world. She had something going on in that big brain of hers.

If it cost Mark his life, so be it. But he would trust she had a plan.

"How did you find us?" He aimed the question at Joaquin. Mark couldn't do much, but maybe he could keep that bastard occupied for a while so he left her alone. "You didn't know about Jenna, you said it yourself. What tipped you off?"

"The man at the hospital you almost caught." Joaquin crossed his arms over his chest. "He was at the hospital observing for a few hours before he failed at his mission to terminate the subject. He reported what he'd seen before he died."

"You killed him?"

Joaquin shook his head. "I didn't. He simply stopped breathing. Amazing how that can happen."

He meant the man had been under subjectification, and he'd let him die and not given him whatever formula was needed to live.

"Naturally, I was intrigued there was someone who'd managed to undo the handiwork my scientists had done, so I began to dig. I discovered Jenna and her tie to Adil Garrison. I decided we needed to meet, so I made that happen."

"Where are we now? Vegas?"

Joaquin's eyes narrowed. "Does it matter?"

Mark shrugged as best he could in the restraints. "I guess not."

The man wasn't going to give him any information, but that didn't mean Mark wasn't going to try.

"I need to use the restroom," Jenna said.

Joaquin stared at her and raised an eyebrow. "Really?"

"Unless you want to spend the next however many hours in a room that smells like a toilet."

He jerked his head at the man who'd brought the food tray. "Take her."

Jenna approached him, and the man tried to grab her arm, but she shrugged it off. Mark couldn't keep the smug satisfaction off his face. The man didn't know she could take him down in a second, regardless of how he was trained.

God, how Mark would laugh if she knocked the guard unconscious and got out of here. He'd be laughing on the way to his grave, but he'd be laughing, nonetheless.

He hoped she would do it, even knowing she wouldn't. Because of him. She wouldn't leave him behind.

Once the door closed, Joaquin turned to him, all pretenses gone. He wasn't the threatening yet charming person trying to get what he wanted. This was the true terrorist.

"If you keep digging, I will gut you, and I won't wait for her to finish her task. I will make it slow. It's your choice, but don't push me."

So they were in Vegas. Joaquin didn't like that Mark had mentioned that. He didn't know that they'd been able to track him and the upcoming sale here.

The Zodiac team was scouring this town right this very second. Didn't mean they would necessarily find him and Jenna, but at least they were searching in the right place.

Mark didn't want to let any of that intel slip. "Your threats are starting to get monotonous."

"You don't know who you're dealing with."

"I know exactly who I'm dealing with, Joaquin Martinez. And by now, I'm sure you know a lot about me too. So, we can do this dance all day, or you can just agree that you're going to try to kill me at the end of it and I'm going to try to kill you if I can."

He needed Joaquin's attention focused more on him than Jenna. Give her a chance to do whatever she was going to do.

The other man smirked. "This is going to be fun. Do your worst, Outlaw. That's your nickname, right? But I always win. Remember that."

Mark didn't respond. Joaquin could call himself the winner all day long, but he didn't know how much of a fight Mark could put up, or the friends that were searching for them right this very second.

This wasn't over.

And Mark wouldn't stop fighting for Jenna until he drew his last breath.

Chapter 26

Jenna's hands were shaking.

The last cup of coffee she'd had was long gone, and things were almost ready.

She rubbed her eyes. She *hoped* they were ready. Her brain was like an internet browser with nineteen different tabs open—four of them were frozen, and she had no idea where the music was coming from.

And the lives of untold people—most imminently hers and Mark's—depended on her ability to keep everything in forward motion.

So yeah, she *hoped* this was all going to work the way she planned.

The couple of times she'd gotten Joaquin to let her go to the bathroom, she'd done her best to observe the layout of the building they were in. To her relief, it didn't seem to be overly complicated. She hadn't seen any stairs or signs of the building being multiple levels. There weren't many windows either.

They were in a lab. Lab buildings didn't tend to be

geared toward comfort or aesthetics; they were all about functionality.

Thankfully, even the buildings terrorists owned needed to be built to regulation, so there were a couple of exit signs, though she hadn't seen the doors.

She would find those once she made her move. And worry about dealing with her panic once she was outside.

First, the formula. It had been ready for the last hour, although she hadn't let Joaquin know. She'd been trying to test it again and again to make sure this version of the universal subjectification compound was truly temporary.

If not, she'd be handing Joaquin the very thing he'd asked for. The process of putting someone under subjectification was relatively simple. Keeping them there was the hard part. People's bodies metabolized the formula quickly, so the real art of it was finding the correct chemical compounds and genetic editing sequence for the subject—which had always been too individualized to be effective on a large scale.

The formula she was staring at now would put anyone under subjectification, but it wouldn't keep them there. About thirty minutes after they were injected, it would wear off and render the person completely whole and themselves, with no memory loss or withdrawal symptoms.

Jenna went over the formula again, running simulations on the computer. There would be no room for trial and error once she gave it to Joaquin. If she got it wrong—if it didn't work or wore off too early—Joaquin would shoot first and ask questions later.

Even worse, shoot *Mark*.

He hadn't tried to talk her out of it again. She hoped he'd understood her cryptic message and was trusting her. But every time she'd looked at him over the last couple of hours, he'd had his eyes closed.

His leg wound was bleeding again. Not a good sign. But right now, she had to focus on the formula.

It was right. It had to be. Over eleven hours had passed, and her brain was fried. There was nothing else she could possibly think to do except to ask someone for outside verification. And that wasn't an option.

So she glanced through the documentation one more time and sent it to the machine to be synthesized.

Joaquin had come back in a few minutes ago. His eyes were harder, posture more tense.

He wasn't screwing around anymore. If this compound didn't work, she and Mark would pay the price.

"Okay," she said, drawing the eyes of Joaquin, who was sitting across the room. "It's being synthesized."

He checked his watch. "And you said you couldn't do it in twelve hours. It's only been eleven."

"It's going to take a while to synthesize."

"Good, then it will still be ready, and we can test it." He looked at her. "Do you have any objections to testing it?"

Mark's eyes opened from where he still sat, bound to the chair. She wanted to go to him, to help him. But mostly just to touch him and draw from his strength.

"You know I have issues with you using this or testing it on anyone. But that's not going to stop you."

"You're correct." He stood. "When I test it, is it going to work?"

"It should," she said. "I've done what I can."

The smallest smile sent chills down her spine. "Well, you know what happens if it doesn't."

She leaned on the table heavily. "I have done everything you asked. The least you can do is admit that and release Mark to go to the fucking bathroom."

"The least I can do is nothing," Joaquin said. "Which is what I'm doing right now. I already told you the rest depends on you. So we'll wait and see what happens, won't we?"

Jenna sat down and looked at Mark. His eyes were closed again, and she could see the tension in his body. She didn't know if peripheral neuropathy got worse with extended periods of stillness—she hadn't had time to do any additional research—but she didn't imagine that made it better. Sitting still that long, his legs were probably numb, hands too, with how tight those restraints were.

She walked to the corner of the lab and slid to the floor. How many times had she sat like this when Garrison held her captive? Trying to make herself small, almost overwhelmed by her own helplessness.

She'd done what she could. Now she had to wait and pray the compound worked the way she planned.

And try to find an opportunity to get them out of this.

The machine beeped, and things were complete.

"Get it ready," Joaquin said, striding to the doors. "Prepare two doses."

Her stomach fell, but Jenna got up and did as he asked. If she could get Mark free, it would be okay.

Joaquin came back with a couple of his men in tow, just as she was finishing preparation of the two doses, and pointed at Mark. "Give him one of the doses."

Jenna froze. She was as certain as she could be that this compound would work the way she intended, but that didn't mean she wanted it tested on Mark.

"No. Use someone else. His body is under too much stress as it is."

Joaquin stalked over to her and yanked the syringes out

of her hands. He pushed her over to his men. "Make sure she doesn't do anything stupid."

One grabbed her arm. She tried to shrug him off, but it didn't work. His fingers dug harder into her arm—hard enough to leave a bruise. She could break his hold easily, but she chose not to. Revealing her martial arts skills now would only get her bound as tightly as Mark was.

"Please don't," she said just before the needle went into Mark's neck.

Mark wasn't moving, breath coming fast, trying to keep himself still.

"Why?" Joaquin raised an eyebrow. "Would you have changed something in the formula if you'd known it was him we would test it on?"

"No," she whispered. "It's right."

"Then there's nothing to worry about, is there?" Joaquin pushed the plunger down into Mark's neck. "I mean, except for the fact that your boyfriend is about to become my willing slave."

Jenna watched Mark's eyes go unfocused and glaze over. His body went slack, and everything about the man she loved was gone, replaced by nothing but the vacant stare of a robot.

"That seems about right." Joaquin grinned and jerked his head toward the man not holding Jenna. "Get him up."

The man removed Mark's restraints and dragged him out of the chair. Mark immediately stumbled, collapsing partway to the floor, his legs unable to hold him due to his wounds and being tied up for so long.

Jenna pulled away from the guard holding her to help Mark, but Joaquin held out a hand, and the man yanked her back. It took every bit of willpower she had not to send this asshole to the hospital.

Not yet. It wasn't quite time.

"Stand up and walk around," Joaquin said to Mark. And as if he were some sort of miracle worker, Mark's body obeyed. He stood and walked without any sign of injury or limitation. The chemicals in his brain were overcoming any physical hindrance.

But it wasn't a miracle, and even if Mark couldn't feel the pain due to the subjectification compound, damage was being done to his body.

Jenna swallowed her need to scream at Joaquin. Mark was alive and that was what mattered. If there was one thing they preached at Zodiac Tactical, it was that *survival was the most important thing*. Everything else—including wounds that may cause Mark to walk with a limp for the rest of his life—was secondary.

Joaquin had Mark walk around the room for a few seconds before turning to her. "Looks like it works. But since you could easily have made a formula for Mark alone here, we're going to test it on someone else. Bring her, and let's go."

That was the reason for a second syringe. The man holding Jenna pulled her with him, down the hallways she'd been trying to observe when she could.

"I have the perfect test," Joaquin said, Mark following blindly behind him as they walked. "Rather than kill Mr. Outlawson outright, I thought I might as well make him useful first. I'm going to enjoy this, although I think perhaps you won't, Jenna."

She was pushed through a set of double doors into an open space that looked like a gym. Sparring mats were on the floor, and fitness equipment was along the walls.

The number of dubious stains on the gray mats made her stomach tumble. Blood. Those were all bloodstains. And way too large to be from something like getting punched in the nose.

Those were bloodstains from people who had bled out and most certainly died.

This was either the most brutal training gym in existence, or that wasn't its only function and Joaquin regularly used this as a torture and murder chamber.

A man knelt in the middle of one of the mats, slumped over and bloody. His back was to Jenna, hands bound behind him. He wasn't moving. The only reason Jenna knew he was alive was because he was still upright.

"People have attempted to infiltrate my organization before, but they're always caught. This one was no different. Now he can do me the service of helping fully test your compound before I dismember him entirely and mail him back to wherever he came from."

Joaquin yanked the man's head up and didn't hesitate to shove the needle straight into his neck. It was all Jenna could do not to gasp.

The man's face was bruised almost beyond recognition—nose obviously broken, one eye completely swollen shut, face and neck covered in blood. She saw the flare of both recognition and relief before he was gone and the eye she could see turned lifeless.

It was Callum.

Chapter 27

Everything was hazy. Mark's thoughts seemed to slip past him before he could fully catch them. Like his mind was a glossy stream, always flowing, shining in the sun with no other thoughts but to keep going and coming back to the start.

Smooth, shining, and peaceful.

There was nothing he had to worry about except the Voice. When he heard it, he would listen. Until then, he was content to stay where he was in the stream.

His legs and arms felt strange and sluggish, but also tingling painfully. There was a reason why, but he didn't fully remember.

Didn't need to remember. Just float.

A man knelt in front of him, and Mark felt the shimmer of recognition in his mind before it slipped away. He didn't know the man. Why would he know him? There was nothing to know except the Voice, and he would listen to it.

"Now, we wait," the Voice said. "To make sure they don't have bad reactions before the second stage of the test."

"Second stage?"

Again, a ping of recognition in his mind at the sound of the woman's voice. Stronger this time. His body wanted to turn toward hers, but there wasn't a reason why. He stayed where he was, staring ahead toward the kneeling man.

"Of course," the Voice said. "I'm sure it comes as no surprise that I don't trust you, Jenna."

Jenna.

He remembered the name, but the meaning of it floated away on the stream. Other voices spoke, and the woman's voice, but they didn't penetrate. Minutes slipped past, brushing against his skin. It was disorienting and made him feel like he was falling while he was standing still.

Wait…what?

The thought wiggled out of his grasp, and he was again nothing but a vessel for the Voice and his commands. But there was something…

"Outlawson," the Voice said, and his mind snapped to attention. "Webb."

The man across from him leaped to his feet. Mark recognized his name too, but couldn't put any meaning to it. He was bloody and bruised. Mark catalogued the man's weaknesses.

"Fight," the Voice said. "To the last man standing. Fight to kill."

"What?" The woman's voice. "You can't. What does that prove?"

He couldn't fully listen. He and the bloodied man were already circling each other. The way he moved told Mark he wasn't completely vulnerable. He had training.

There were no memories to tell him where his own training came from, but he had some too. The man stepped forward and threw a punch that Mark dodged easily. His legs still felt strange, but the Voice had instructed him to fight, and there was no other option.

He would fight.

But after a few minutes, both taking and giving some blows, it felt wrong. Just for a second.

He didn't want to do this. He didn't want to fight.

But there wasn't anything else for him to do. This was what the Voice had said to do, and that was the end of it. Wasn't it?

He moved, sidestepping his opponent and bringing his elbow up for a strike, and it hit. Pain radiated down his arm, and he backed off.

Why was he doing this?

His thoughts disappeared, sinking below the surface.

Fight to the last man standing.

"They're fighting each other." The woman. "See? I did what you asked. They're obeying you, and they didn't have a bad reaction. Stop this now."

The man came at him and landed a punch to Mark's side. He grunted and blocked, returning the hit, the two of them grappling, struggling for dominance before breaking apart.

Mark saw the gleam of combat in the man's eyes, and it was...*familiar*. As if he'd seen it before. Determination and grit.

As he'd seen when Callum had come to them in Oak Creek.

The thought froze him before it disappeared, allowing his opponent to land a cracking hit against his jaw. He nearly fell, but he got his feet underneath him again, able to retreat to avoid another hit. This felt normal. This felt better.

Fixing his stance, Mark dug in his feet just before Callum crashed into him, sending them both to the floor. It reminded him of when his leg had gone out sparring with Jenna.

Right before he kissed her.

His mind tried to drag the memories into the stream again. Into nothing. But it didn't fully work this time.

There were echoes of his life, and he was clinging to them now even as he swung for Callum's head, missed, and followed up with a combination to his torso.

"Stop playing with each other," the Voice said.

Only it wasn't the Voice. It was Joaquin. Joaquin Martinez. Wasn't it?

Mark had the advantage, but he backed away. His head was spinning and battling itself, trying to return to the state of simple calm and obedience of doing what the Voice told him to.

But the rest of his mind was saying no. *Hell no.*

Fight.

He ducked under Callum's kick and threw his body at him, taking them down to the stained floor mat. They were both making sounds, grunting as they exchanged hits. But within that, he heard the words disguised as sounds of battle.

"Remember. Focus."

Had he said that? Had Callum?

They rolled apart and came to their feet. With every passing second, Mark's mind was coming back to him more and more. He tried to keep his focus singular and make it seem like he was still under the effect of the drugs.

The compound. A robot.

Mark was supposed to be a robot under Joaquin's control right now, but he was coming out of it on his own.

Jenna.

Trust me.

Jenna had done this. Jenna had changed the compound so it wasn't permanent. That was what she'd been working on all day.

Callum's eyes were clear too. They couldn't show it yet, but they circled each other, seemingly fighting, but instead examining who else was in the room. Joaquin, Jenna, and three others.

As soon as they stopped fighting each other, Jenna would fight too. She wasn't bound.

Mark lunged for Callum, landing two punches before grappling together. There was real force behind their struggle, but they turned, lining themselves up to get into position.

"Ready?" Mark gritted the word through his teeth.

Callum nodded and threw the punch at Mark's gut that broke them apart. And together, they turned toward the real enemies.

Chapter 28

Jenna didn't know when Joaquin had discovered that Callum was undercover, but the man looked awful. He needed a hospital. And now, he'd been injected with the compound. His eyes went glassy.

He and Mark would come out from under the effects of the compound at roughly the same time, if they survived that long. They needed to survive that long.

Mark stood in front of Callum, and neither man moved, staring into the space the other occupied without any kind of reaction.

Hang on. Hang on, and I'll get us out of this.

She had to get them all out of this.

"Now, we wait," Joaquin said. "To make sure they don't have bad reactions before the second stage of the test."

Dread pooled in her stomach. "Second stage?"

Joaquin looked at her, and it was clear in the look exactly what he thought of her and that reaction. "Of course. I'm sure it comes as no surprise that I don't trust you, Jenna."

"I haven't given you any reason not to trust me," she

argued. Every minute that passed and every delay she could impose was a good thing.

"Forgive me if I need to be sure." The terrorist's tone was dripping with sarcasm.

The rest of the fifteen minutes were the longest minutes Jenna had ever experienced, apart from those nights she was forced to spend outside. Those had felt like an eternity too.

Joaquin's phone rang. He left the room to take the call, and Jenna tried to pull away from the man holding her. He kept her arm firmly in his grasp. "There's three of you. Do you really think holding on to me like a toddler who won't share a toy is going to help?"

"Shut up," the man said.

She rolled her eyes. "Yes, what a wonderfully well-thought-out response."

The doors burst open, and Joaquin entered again. Something was different. His energy was even sharper than it had been, entirely focused on the two men frozen and held by the formula she created.

"Outlawson." He called. "Webb." Callum rose to his feet, though it was clear he wasn't steady. "Fight. To the last man standing. Fight to kill."

"What?" Jenna's voice echoed through the room almost before she realized that she'd spoken. "You can't. What does that prove?"

They were already moving, the drugs in their system forcing them to obey. From here on out, it would be degrading, and they would eventually fall out from under the compound's control. But both men were lethal, and right now, they were about to go at each other without any remorse and without any mercy.

They could easily kill each other in a few minutes.

Joaquin didn't respond to her outburst. He was watching Mark and Callum as they circled each other. Callum threw a punch, which Mark dodged easily. They were falling into their fighting instincts and were still assessing each other, but she'd sparred with Mark. Neuropathy aside, she knew he was good, and she also knew he would never forgive himself if he killed Callum while he was in a state he couldn't control.

She'd never forgive herself either.

"This has to stop," she said quietly. Again, she pulled away from the man holding her. "This needs to stop."

He yanked her close, now fully holding her and immobilizing her. "I told you to shut up."

She didn't. "They're fighting each other. See?" She yelled the words at Joaquin, even though the man didn't seem like he could hear her at all. "I did what you asked. They're obeying you, and they didn't have a bad reaction. Stop this now."

She winced as Callum got in a brutal punch to Mark's ribs, and then they really started going at each other, both getting blows in. They moved closer, grappling before breaking apart and going back to circle each other.

They didn't stand apart for long. Callum threw himself at Mark and took them both to the floor. Jenna tried to keep herself neutral, but seeing him go down had her heart in her throat. How many minutes had it been? How long until they started to realize they were being forced to do this and stopped?

"Stop playing with each other," Joaquin said.

They were still on the floor, and suddenly, Mark was on top, landing several hits to Callum before he abruptly jumped away. He shook his head like he was trying to clear it, and Jenna did everything in her power not to react.

Come on. Please work.

Callum executed a perfect kick that Mark dodged before tackling him once more. This time, they grunted as they grappled, seemingly losing control and becoming more feral.

They rolled apart and came to their feet. They circled again, and when Jenna looked at Joaquin, all she saw was glee. This was everything he wanted. Two people who didn't share a similar DNA profile, who liked and respected each other, fighting to the death. Entirely under his complete and utter control. Willing to kill someone else because their entire personhood was erased.

Mark took the advantage this time, lunging for Callum, and the sound of fists hitting made her sick. She had to do something. If the compound didn't begin to wear off in the next minute, either Callum or Mark would end up dead.

She could fight.

She *would* fight.

It was a long shot, but maybe she could take out Joaquin and his men before they could pull their guns. Then knock both Mark and Callum unconscious so they didn't kill each other.

The chances were slim, so very slim, but she had to try.

She couldn't sit there and do nothing while the man she loved was killed or killed someone else.

She looked down to find her own hand shaking. She didn't feel like she could take anyone on right now. Where was the woman who'd put a stranger in the hospital just because he'd happened to touch her shoulder the wrong way?

She'd forced that woman so far down inside her psyche that maybe she didn't exist anymore. Maybe the only thing she could hit with any power were the BOBs in her gym.

Maybe she was useless.

No.

What you can do is all you can do.

She heard Mark's voice clear in her mind. She wasn't useless.

And if she was going out, she was going out fighting. Not crying, not cowering, like she'd done for way too long.

She was about to make her move when she saw where Mark's hand was wrapped around Callum's neck and froze. There was no pressure. Callum's skin wasn't tight, and there was no force behind Mark's grip. His eyes flicked to hers and back.

That simple motion alone had relief pouring through her at the same time she was strengthening her stance, grounding her feet to the floor, waiting for the change.

Her plan had worked, and now they just had to survive the aftermath. She would do whatever she had to do to ensure that happened.

Suddenly, both Callum and Mark snapped apart and leaped straight for the two guards. Jenna moved, throwing her hips back into the man who held her to throw him off-balance before slamming her foot down onto his so hard it didn't matter what kind of shoes he was wearing, she broke his foot.

Rage burned under her skin as he released her, and she turned, unleashing everything she'd always tried to keep carefully locked down. He was still off-balance, and a punch to the throat had him falling back.

Jenna was barely conscious of the moves she was executing, only knowing that she was making them. She felt the crack of bone under her hands, and the man was on the floor fully unconscious, face slack with it.

Joaquin was halfway to the doors. Mark and Callum were still fighting their respective guards.

It wasn't a decision. She ran, throwing herself onto the man's back just before he reached the double doors, slamming him into them and taking them both down to the floor.

He landed on top of her with his full weight, knocking the air from her lungs, and pain fogged everything for a brief second. Joaquin rolled, and she followed, landing a blow to the side of his head.

The man was bigger than her in every way possible. But she'd learned long ago that size meant nothing with the right leverage. All she had to do was find it.

"And you wonder why I said I didn't trust you," Joaquin growled, grabbing her and tossing her away from him in order to get to his feet. "You're a brilliant woman, and with the right motivation, we could have done some great things together. It's a pity."

He swung at her, and she ducked and spun, landing a quick jab to his kidney. She had nothing to say to him. The arrogant ass was only wasting breath in the middle of a fight.

She continued to dart around him, and out of the corner of her eye, she saw the other men go down under Mark's and Callum's fists. Callum surged forward to help her, but Mark put one hand to his chest, and a single flashing glance at his face told her she had this and he knew it.

This was her fight.

She let the beast inside her free. For every time she'd been forced to do something against her will. For every life that had been lost because of it. For the arrogance of people like Adil Garrison and Joaquin Martinez who thought that money was more valuable than human lives.

For the fact that she was never going to walk on the beach ever again.

The beast inside her raged.

Jenna was fast, but Joaquin was strong. She blocked the blows she could and took the ones she couldn't.

Spinning behind him, she leaped, using her elbow to slam down into the place where his shoulder met his neck. His roar of pain was music to her, and she took him the rest of the way down, wrapping her legs around his neck and squeezing. She held one of his arms, so he couldn't move.

For the first time since she'd met him, Joaquin Martinez had no fucking leverage.

He almost managed to shove her off, but she held fast, and the words of abuse he was hurling at her faded as he slumped beneath her, unconscious.

They'd done it.

She felt when he passed out, and she relaxed, scrambling away. Now that it was over, she didn't want to touch him in any capacity.

Callum was already there, getting Joaquin's phone, and Mark was pulling her to her feet.

"We've got to get out of here," Callum said. "There're a lot more fucking people in this building than the four of them."

"Are we in Vegas?" Mark asked.

Callum nodded, dialing a number on the phone as they moved toward the door. A few seconds later, he actually smiled. "Looks like help is already on the way. Ian and the Zodiac team are about to infiltrate. They'd already pinpointed our location. Thanks to some ping Jenna put out."

Mark looked at her, eyebrow raised. She shrugged. "Their closed system wasn't as closed as they thought it was. I got an encrypted message out to Kendrick Foster of Linear Tactical. But I wasn't sure if he got it or would recognize it for what it was. I especially didn't expect it this early."

The power blew, and the gym of horrors fell into darkness. The noise of firearms could be heard in the hallway.

They had done it.

Chapter 29

Mark had forgotten how grueling a debriefing could be. Granted, having a knife wound didn't help. He'd given quite a bit of his statement while an ER doc stitched him up.

He'd be on crutches for a while and would need physical therapy to rebuild the muscle damage in his leg from Joaquin's little knife gift, but it would ultimately heal. He was much better off than Callum, who'd basically collapsed from his wounds as soon as the Zodiac team arrived. Callum was stable, but with a broken nose, multiple cracked ribs, a concussion, and internal bleeding, the man wouldn't be leaving the hospital for a while.

Mark had told his account of the events to damned near everybody—local law enforcement, Callum's colleagues at Omega Sector, Ian and the Zodiac team. Hell, even Jenna's brother had been there. Mark had told Craig what happened too, even though he wasn't there in an official FBI capacity.

He'd wanted to know that his sister was okay. Mark wished the other man could've seen her kick Joaquin's ass. That would've reassured him that he'd done the right thing by asking for Jenna's help at the start.

By the time Mark was done, it was nearly midnight. There were hotel rooms for them to stay, and he knew Jenna had already gone back to hers. He'd wanted to escort her himself, but carrying her wouldn't be possible for some time.

But she'd been surviving the outside dash without him for a while, so he knew she could do it when she had to. Maybe beating Joaquin to a pulp would help make it a little easier.

But Mark didn't fool himself into believing Jenna was cured. This wasn't the movies; it didn't work that way. Like his peripheral neuropathy, Jenna would be dealing with her agoraphobia for the rest of her life.

And it was his intention to be at her side to help her every time she needed to go outside for as long as she would let him.

He knocked on her hotel room door, hoping she was awake, but he also wanted her to be sleeping. She deserved it.

Still, the sound of her footsteps after his light knock set butterflies loose in his chest.

Jenna answered the door in nothing but an oversized Linear Tactical T-shirt, and everything he'd wanted to say went out the window. He wasn't sure who moved first—whether he pushed through the door or Jenna tugged him inside. But it didn't matter. He tossed the crutches aside and pulled her to him. Their mouths met, hot and hungry, as the door clicked shut.

He was breathless when he finally lifted his mouth from hers. "Believe it or not, I'd actually planned on just talking."

"I'm happy to talk," she said, more than a little breathless herself. "As long as you don't stop touching me."

"Wouldn't dream of it, little librarian."

He left the crutches where they were and limped toward

the bed, dragging her with him. They tumbled onto it together, and he brushed her hair away from her face. It was still damp from her shower, and in the dim light of the room, she was the most beautiful thing he'd ever seen. He didn't think there would be a time when he got tired of looking at her.

"I love you," he said softly. "I wanted to say it the second we got out of that lab today, but I didn't want to have an audience for it. I love you, and I'm so grateful we're alive so I can tell you that."

"I love you too." Her eyes were glassy, and she ducked her head, tucking it beneath his chin as he gathered her closer. "I was really scared."

"You were amazing on every possible level. Tricking Joaquin and altering the subjectification compound? Getting word out to Zodiac so they could find us? Absolutely incredible."

She smiled.

"But most especially, turning yourself loose and kicking Joaquin's ass. That is going to be a source of wet dreams like I'm some damned teenager."

She laughed, and he pulled back far enough to kiss her, taking advantage of her hot, open mouth. They didn't stop, falling into each other for a while.

When they broke apart, his heart was pounding and his head was buzzing. Damned if Mark wouldn't rather kiss this woman than breathe.

He lay back on the bed, pulling her close to his side. Neither of them was in any shape to make love tonight, but just having her close was enough for him. "Did you get to talk to Craig?"

"Yeah. He was upset that things had gotten so out of control. I think he honestly thought all my assistance would be from behind a computer. Of course, I thought that too, so

I can't blame him. He's going to come to Oak Creek next week so the two of us can really talk."

"Good. That'll be good for both of you. We've been cleared to leave tomorrow to go home."

"I'm so ready."

"And what about me?" He had to ask. "Do you want me to come back to Oak Creek full time?"

She leaned up on one elbow so they could see each other's faces. "There are…things I'm worried about."

"Like what?"

Her whole body went stiff, and he ran his hands down her spine, immediately trying to soothe her.

"Like I love you. And I know we haven't talked about this at all and I may be completely jumping the gun, but I don't think I can ever get married and have kids. What will I tell them when they're in T-ball games and Mom can't go watch them because it's outside?"

This woman. Her giant brain got her out of so much trouble, but it also trapped her sometimes. Kept her prisoner because it was considering so many scenarios to the nth degree.

He kissed her on the nose. "Let's not worry about kids yet. And for the record, I'm perfectly happy without them, or happy figuring out how to manage everything if we do have kids. Let's not skip to the end just yet."

She bit her lip in a way that was entirely adorable. "Okay."

"Good."

She glared at him, though he could tell it wasn't serious. "But you're not moving in with me right away, Outlaw. Just because I love you doesn't mean I don't want to be romanced."

"Don't worry." Mark shifted them so she was underneath his body. "I plan on romancing the fuck out of you."

She rolled her eyes. "Good start."

"I thought so."

So much for not being in any shape to have sex. They folded into each other, finally letting all the talking fall behind. Mark showed Jenna how much he loved her, and how much he wanted to love her every second for the rest of their lives.

When she was collapsed onto his chest, sleepily catching her breath, he pulled her even closer. "I love you, little librarian."

"Love you too." The quiet words stirred things in him, and he breathed with her until she was fast asleep.

Gently, he extricated himself from her and put on some clothes, grabbing his crutches. It was late, but he was making a bet that Ian was still awake. He needed to talk to him, and then he would be back with Jenna and not leave her side.

His wager was correct. Ian was still working, going through the debriefing statements and watching a feed of Joaquin being questioned in a holding room.

Ian looked up when he saw Mark "Everything okay? I thought you would be with Jenna."

"I was and will be again in a few minutes. But remember when you said whatever I needed to get situated in a new career, you'd help?"

The man smiled. "I do. What do you need?"

Mark closed the door behind him. "I need a favor."

Epilogue

Three months later

"One date," Mark said, sitting beside her on the couch. It was something he'd been asking for weeks now, and her frustration grew.

"Mark, please."

"Jenna," he said. "I'm serious. I want to take you on a date."

She stood, putting the bowl of popcorn on the coffee table, and crossed her arms over her chest, pacing. "I don't understand why you keep asking that. You know how I feel about going out. The only thing a date would be is stressful and terrible, and I don't really feel like throwing up my guts just to spend time with you outside of this house. Why can't we stay here where everything is comfortable and fine?"

This was what she'd been afraid of. That Mark would get frustrated with her when she wasn't getting any *better*. She was never going to get better. At least not enough to go out on *dates*.

She had a horrible feeling that this was the beginning of the end.

And an even worse feeling that Mark leaving would succeed in doing what Garrison and Joaquin had both failed to do: completely break her.

She stopped pacing and glared at Mark. "If you don't understand what that will do to me after all this time—"

Mark stood and held out his hands. "Do you trust me?"

Did she trust him? That was the real question. It was a yes or no answer, but somehow it felt much bigger than that.

"I— Yes. Yes, I trust you."

"Then why would you think I would drag you somewhere that would terrorize you?"

She shrugged and looked at the floor. "Because that's what dates are. Out in public, around people. Requiring me to go outside."

Slowly, he pulled her into his arms, and she let him. "Give me one date," he whispered against her hair. "Trust me, and I promise you by the end of it, I'll have proven that I understand you."

"That's a big promise."

"I'm a confident guy."

She pulled back and looked at him, and nothing about his face said that he was teasing her. He wanted to take her on this date, and she knew Mark wouldn't hurt her.

"Fine."

"Thank you," he said, brushing a kiss across her forehead. "We'll go tomorrow."

"Go where?"

"I'm keeping it a surprise."

She grumbled as she sat back down on the couch and cuddled into his side. "I don't like surprises."

She liked to be prepared. She liked to research so she

could run all the scenarios in her head and prep for each one.

"I think you'll like this one." His phone beeped, and he pulled it from his pocket and checked. "Good."

"What?"

"Zac Mackay and Finn Bollinger reviewed the plans for one of the new buildings over at Linear, and they like it."

"That is good," she agreed.

Mark was no longer a bodyguard. Instead, he now worked at Linear Tactical, assisting as an instructor in their self-defense and situational awareness classes. But that was secondary to his primary role—designing and overseeing the expansion of the Linear Tactical mission to include raising and training service animals for people suffering from PTSD.

Like their friends at the Resting Warrior Ranch in Montana, Zac and Finn and the other Linear guys wanted to branch out in this new direction. Mark was using his architecture and engineering skills to help draw up the new buildings that would be needed. Ones for humans and animals.

The job was long-term and perfect, given his condition meant he couldn't always teach. But he did when he could, and it took the edge off having to give up bodyguard work.

Though he regularly claimed he would always be her bodyguard.

"I love you," he whispered into her hair. She never got tired of hearing the words, and neither of them would ever take them for granted after what they'd been through.

But still, this date? She couldn't help but think it might be the beginning of their end.

"Is this okay to wear for where we're going?"

Jenna had on jeans and a T-shirt, but Mark had stubbornly not given her any clues about where he was taking her on this *date*. Her stomach was a whole mess of anxiety, and the thought of getting more dressed up than this was making it worse.

"That's perfect."

"Really?"

"Really," he laughed. "Ready to go?"

"No."

He took her hand and pulled her to the garage, helping her into the car and kissing her long and hard before shutting her door. His door was shut and locked as well before the garage ever opened. If they could just stay like this, everything would be fine.

"You're really not going to give me any clues?"

"You'll see in a minute." Mark was all smiles. "I promise you'll know as soon as you see it."

She crossed her arms and did her best to try to look happy.

And failed miserably.

But the truth was, she was curious, and she did trust Mark. If he said he wasn't trying to push her past what she was capable of, she needed to believe him.

And he was right. She knew as soon as she saw it.

In a field on the outskirts of town, a giant screen had been set up, and already images and advertisements were flashing on it. A whole array of cars were parked in the field in front of it and, in front of them, people on picnic blankets waiting for the movie.

It looked like nearly everyone in Oak Creek had come out to a makeshift drive-in movie.

Mark pulled the SUV into one of the spots and put it in park. When he looked over, his smile rivaled the sun. "See? No getting out of the car." He reached behind him and pulled a bag from the back seat, and Jenna laughed when she saw it was filled with classic movie candy. "And I definitely think this qualifies as a date."

"It does." Tears pricked her eyes. "It really does. I'm sorry I didn't trust you the way I should."

He leaned across the car and kissed her. "Don't be sorry. But I want you to know that I'm with you, whatever you need. I want to live a life with you. Will it be different from most people's lives? Definitely. That doesn't bother me. Especially since my neuropathy means the same thing for you from the opposite side. I think we both owe it to ourselves not to let potential difficulties stop us."

"You're right." She breathed the words against his lips. "You're right."

"And now, for the second surprise."

Jenna raised her eyebrows. "There's another one?"

"I told you I was going to prove I understood you, and I think this will help."

What he pulled out next from the back seat did surprise her. A rolled-up piece of paper like a scroll, that she recognized immediately as building plans. She'd seen enough of them in the last few months to know. "What is it?"

"Take a look."

It was a little awkward in the car, but she unfurled the blueprints and tried to decipher them in the fading light of the sunset.

A house?

She slowly took in the details, and something clicked. There were two rooms on the second floor that seemed familiar. A pair of connected rooms, and the elevations made them look simple and beautiful. A pair of offices, just like the ones they'd talked about together on the plane.

"Mark, what is this?"

"A safe house," he said quietly. "*Our* safe house. Our *permanent* safe house."

"You—" There was too much emotion in the back of her throat for her to get out the words she wanted.

Mark reached over and turned the pages. "It will have the library you wanted, the offices we talked about, a basement fortress, and an elevator in case there's ever a time I can't manage the stairs. Every security measure known to humankind, and probably the most important, it's invisible."

"What do you mean?"

"Ian told me that whatever I needed, he'd help with. And as much as I wish there were no more men like Garrison or Joaquin, there are."

Jenna nodded. She would always be in some kind of danger even if they took every precaution. Now that the knowledge of what she could do was out there, someone might try to exploit it.

"I told him I needed a favor, and he came through. About a month ago, Zodiac Tactical purchased a very large parcel of land on the edge of the mountains not too far from here. There are contracts in place, so the land belongs to me, but neither of our names will ever be attached to it. I want to build this into the side of the mountain, and maybe even expand the existing mining tunnels there for ways to get you into town without having to go outside."

She stared at him for long moments, completely and utterly speechless. And then she launched herself at him, not caring if she was crushing the blueprints between them. She needed to kiss this man more than she needed her next breath.

"I love it," she said. "I love it and I love you and it's perfect."

"I'm glad you like it."

"A whole hell of a lot more than like it."

Mark drew his hand down her face. "I know you're not sure about marriage or family. But this is that for me—a commitment to you and our life together, no matter what happens."

She blinked away tears and smoothed the blueprints out over her lap. No matter what happened. They were both losing parts of themselves they couldn't get back, but as long as they faced the world together, everything would be okay. She knew that now, as deeply as she could know something.

"No matter what happens," she said.

Mark rolled up the blueprints, and in front of them, the movie began to play on the big screen. She was going to need to make a modification to this car and turn the front seat into a convertible couch immediately, because this would not be the last time they did this.

Their date options would always be limited. But not impossible. Between the two of them, she didn't think anything was impossible.

He turned and kissed her temple, inhaling her in that way he had that always made her shiver. "You and me. No matter what the future holds."

Bonus Epilogue

Ten years later

"Mom! Mom! Did you see me score my goal?"

Jenna gritted her teeth as her six-year-old daughter opened the door to the minivan and jumped inside, hand in hand with her bestie, River Bollinger.

Mark was right behind them. Jenna relaxed as he quickly shut the door once they were all inside.

For ten years, he'd been closing doors quickly for her. He never tested her, never tried to push her to keep the door open and tough it out.

And she loved the man just as much for it now as she had at the beginning.

She pulled Megan in for a hug. "You know I saw it! I watched the whole game!"

Megan grinned, her green eyes so much like her father's squinting at the screen in front of Jenna. "Show me, show me!"

Mark smiled and handed Megan and River juice boxes as Jenna pulled up the footage of the goal.

Jenna had been wrong. She'd been wrong about so many things all those years ago when she told Mark it couldn't work-long term between them.

She'd been wrong to think Mark would tire of dealing with her agoraphobia.

She'd been wrong to think she couldn't have a family and participate actively in their lives.

She'd been wrong to think her friends in Oak Creek would demand more than she could give.

Case in point, the fact that Charlie Bollinger had been sitting in the van with Jenna for the game—cooler full of *medicinal* beers to ensure they survived the tedium of watching six-year-olds attempt soccer. As she had every game this season.

And that was just the tip of the iceberg when it came to Jenna's friends.

They'd built an overhang at the back door of the Eagle's Nest so she could walk from her vehicle into the building without fear overtaking her, giving her a place to go out whenever she wanted.

They set up the pop-up drive-in movie location outside of town every single weekend in the summer so she could hang out with everyone.

They'd piled into her and Mark's new house for their wedding eight years ago—determined she would have a stress-free day she could enjoy and they could participate in.

They'd gone out of their way to make sure she was included and comfortable. Because they were family. Not related by blood, but by something more important: choice.

She chose these people, and they chose her right back.

They'd helped her when Mark's peripheral neuropathy had taken a turn for the worse just after Megan was born and Jenna needed help. And celebrated with them when he'd gotten better.

And not a single one of them demanded a thing in return, although she and Mark had tried to do their part too. Mark had worked tirelessly designing and building the expansion of Linear Tactical. Jenna continued to use her talent with computers to assist where needed.

Including teaching the elementary school kids in town computer basics via video call each week. Not only how to use their electronics, but how recognize and report predators who might attempt to prey on them. Chemical subjectification wasn't the only means of human trafficking, and Jenna would do whatever she could to keep the next generation safe.

"I didn't score a goal, Mommy," River said, slumping onto her mother's lap.

Charlie hugged her. "Next time, kid. Don't worry, your turn is coming."

Megan nodded solemnly. "We'll keep practicing, Riv. Don't worry."

River's eyes lit up. "And Ethan and Jess will be home in a couple weeks. He'll help too!"

Both girls jumped up and did a little dance in the middle of the decked-out minivan. Ethan was older than his baby sister by nearly twenty years and was a former Navy SEAL. In River's mind, he and his wife Jess could do no wrong. Evidently, soccer included.

Charlie grinned over at Jenna. "I'll have Ethan and Jess as built-in babysitters. I love it."

The girls squealed as Jenna cued up the footage and they were able to watch Megan's goal. Then back it up and watch it again.

After the girls' seventh time doing a victory dance, Charlie called a stop to the insanity.

"Okay, Bollinger, time to go."

"Aw, Mom, not yet!" River made a comedically tragic face. "Can Megan have a sleepover?"

Charlie rolled her eyes and looked over at Jenna. "Up to you. She's welcome, as always."

"Please, Mommy? Please?" Megan pleaded with giant green eyes. "That way you and Daddy can have your special time downstairs."

Charlie snickered.

"Fine," Jenna said with an exaggerated sigh. "Go have your fun. I guess I'll hang out with Dad if I have to."

With squeals of excitement and hugs all around, Charlie led the girls out of the van.

As soon as the door closed behind them, Mark pulled Jenna onto his lap. "I'm looking forward to *special time* with you downstairs."

She spun until she was straddling his hips. She ran her fingers through his hair over his ears. This man. He'd been everything to her from their first kiss.

He would be everything to her until their last one.

"I think I want *special time* with you upstairs first."

Special time downstairs was sparring. Upstairs was… whatever they wanted and needed.

Which was always each other.

He pulled her closer until their lips were touching. "Both."

Her eyes closed at the familiar pressure of his lips against hers. She would never tire of this. Of him.

Of *them*.

"Both. Forever and always."

•••

Acknowledgments

A very special thanks to the Calamittie Jane Publishing editing and proofreading team:

    Denise Hendrickson
    Susan Greenbank
    Chasidy Brooks
    Tesh Elborne
    Marilize Roos
    Lisa at Silently Correcting Your Grammar

Thank you for your ongoing dedication for making these romantic suspense books the best they can be.

And to the creative minds at Deranged Doctor Designs who fashioned all the covers for this series and made the books so beautiful—thank you!

Also by Janie Crouch

All books: https://www.janiecrouch.com/books

LINEAR/ZODIAC TACTICAL CROSSOVER
Code Name: OUTLAW

ZODIAC TACTICAL (series complete)
Code Name: ARIES

Code Name: VIRGO

Code Name: LIBRA

Code Name: PISCES

RESTING WARRIOR RANCH (with Josie Jade)
Montana Sanctuary

Montana Danger

Montana Desire

Montana Mystery

Montana Storm

Montana Freedom

Montana Silence

LINEAR TACTICAL SERIES (series complete)
Cyclone

Eagle

Shamrock

Angel

Ghost

Shadow

Echo

Phoenix

Baby

Storm

Redwood

Scout

Blaze

Forever

INSTINCT SERIES (series complete)

Primal Instinct

Critical Instinct

Survival Instinct

THE RISK SERIES (series complete)

Calculated Risk

Security Risk

Constant Risk

Risk Everything

OMEGA SECTOR SERIES (series complete)

Stealth

Covert

Conceal

Secret

OMEGA SECTOR: CRITICAL RESPONSE (series complete)

About the Author (Janie Crouch)

"Passion that leaps right off the page." - Romantic Times Book Reviews

USA Today and Publishers Weekly bestselling author Janie Crouch writes what she loves to read: passionate romantic suspense featuring protective heroes. Her books have won multiple awards, including the Romance Writers of America's coveted Vivian® Award, the National Readers Choice Award, and the Booksellers' Best.

After a lifetime on the East Coast, and a six-year stint in Germany due to her husband's job as support for the U.S. Military, Janie has settled into her dream home in Front Range of the Colorado Rockies.

When she's not listening to the voices in her head—and even when she is—she enjoys engaging in all sorts of crazy adventures (200-mile relay races; Ironman Triathlons, treks to Mt. Everest Base Camp...), traveling, and hanging out with her four kids.

Her favorite quote: "Life is a daring adventure or nothing." ~ Helen Keller.

facebook.com/janiecrouch

amazon.com/author/janiecrouch

instagram.com/janiecrouch

bookbub.com/authors/janie-crouch

Printed in the USA
CPSIA information can be obtained
at www.ICGtesting.com
LVHW051118280324
775734LV00002B/112